IT'S Not Only Love…

JEETENDRA WADHWANI

FROG BOOKS

ISBN 978-93-52010-04-2
Copyright © Jeetendra Wadhwani, 2019

First published in India 2019 by Frog Books
An imprint of Leadstart Publishing Pvt Ltd

Sales Office:
Unit No.25/26, Building No.A/1,
Near Wadala RTO,
Wadala (East), Mumbai – 400037 India
Phone: +91 22 24046887
Email: info@leadstartcorp.com
www.leadstartcorp.com

Disclaimer: The Views expressed in this book are those of the
Author and do not pertain to be held by the Publisher.

Editor: Shayoni Mitra
Cover: Dhiraj
Layouts: Victor Patali

DEDICATION

I'm grateful to all the people I've associated with during my career in the industry across various organizations including but not restricted to bosses, peers, juniors, support department personnel as well as service providers. I've been sufficiently enriched by the experiences of various people to come up with this story.

Beside them, I've been moved by various stories on how numerous established best-selling authors took up writing – as well as people who would make the unlikeliest of candidates for certain jobs and thus began to attempt something of this scale.

Lastly but not the very bit least, I would like to sincerely thank my family for their support, encouragement and standing by me in this journey of coming up with this story.

Disclaimer

All characters, situations, behaviors and organisations in this tale are fictional and are a work of imagination. Any resemblances to any persons, circumstances, bodies or actions are purely coincidental and are not intended to outrage, insult, hurt or tarnish any group of people, religion or establishment; nor to promote any sentiments, beliefs, or ideas and are solely for entertainment purposes.

ABOUT THE AUTHOR

Mr. Jeetendra Wadhwani, an M.B.A. & M.COM, has previously served as a senior technocrat for 15 years in the Information Technology industry and has worked for some of the major software companies like PCS, Satyam. For the past 10 years, he had been running his own training business, imparting language, speech and communication based services to various functions.

Following are his contact details:

Facebook: Author.rises   Instagram: author.rises

Twitter: AuthorRises   Gmail: author.rises

PREFACE

This tale traces the passage of Tushar, Harry, Sunny & Maitri from their childhood schooling days to their adolescent college days, right up to their working years. They meet new friends with some of them becoming a part of their voyage. They grow up with each other at various stages of their work and lives – learning to cope with everything that it throws at them with various lessons.

While bouquets are gently presented, it's the brickbats that are thrust on them. See whether their decisions help them rule or make them rue it all their lives. Conflicts might either bring them even closer together or threaten to scatter them completely apart. See how they explore the meaning of their lives and how they traverse this journey with a lot of fun and games – even though life isn't quite so.

CONTENTS

Acknowledgements

The background to this writing voyage of mine started while being a technocrat working in the software industry when factors like industry turmoil coupled with personal setbacks moved me to do what my heart always desired. And Voila! What I intended to do in the near future now became my newer present. From working out of a desk, it made me create that desk in my mind. The love for and musing of the industry is what truly veered me to start this passage with a story set in it. Along the way, it also enabled me to pursue other sought after interests – in addition to giving my family some much needed attention.

The real motivation behind this interactive writing style has been the celebrated author Arthur Miller's drama adaptation of his renowned play 'A View from the Bridge'.

1

THIS USED TO BE MY PLAYGROUND

What have we here? We've got four friends who are studying in one of the premier primary high schools of Mumbai. They're Tushar, Harish, Sunny and Maitri. This is Tushar – an impulsive kid and that's Sunny – a thinking child. While their natures are only as similar as chalk and cheese, they share common tastes in shakes and shoes. Here's Maitri – a careful little girl who's alert to all the mischief that goes around while that one's Harish or Harry – as they call him – because he's always in a *hurry* and no – not because he's *dirty (harry)*. Maitri on her part does all her homework and so does Harry, but the only difference being while Harry would do it just about anywhere in the notebook, Maitri would be little miss prim and proper.

Fed up of the constant heckling from Sunny and Tushar, MAITRI said to both of them (threateningly): "Please stop teasing me or I'll tell your names to miss."

SUNNY (boldly): "Go *na* (then). But she already knows it" as Tushar bursts out laughing.

HARRY: "Stop it, you nosy parkers."

TUSHAR: "So then you people must be *Sheaffers*" and Sunny laughs out aloud at his pun on *pens*, much to Harry's dismay.

MAITRI: "I'll complain to miss about you cheater-cocks."

TUSHAR: "Harry, don't shake your head like a fighter-*cock*."

HARRY (enraged): "No, you –."

SUNNY (cutting him off): "If we're cocks, then you must surely be *pigs* with all this squealing..." They both walk away chuckling.

MAITRI (excitedly): "Let's play jolly with our pens" but the boys just didn't show any interest.

(Continuing) "Ok then, how about 'name, place, animal, thing'?" to which they give a jaded look.

TUSHAR: "Now don't say fish pond, else we'll throw you into a small *pond*."

SUNNY: "Maitri, how about dog and the bone?"

MAITRI: "Here, in the class?"

SUNNY (smirking): "Yes – why not? You'll play the dog and we'll throw the bone for you to fetch." As the boys burst out laughing much to her dismay, she proceeded to cream him while he tried his best to evade her.

What I couldn't fathom is that – though the school is at a low slope or level – why is it still called *high* school? Anyways, our dear friends keep having their daily run-ins while *running* around.

MAITRI (sobbing): "Why did you hit me, Tushar?" while the boys chuckle away at that.

TUSHAR (responding): "You forgot to say 'hops' before standing up" as he smiles at her naivety while playing the ancient Indian game hops and bats.

MAITRI: "I'm not playing that game with you. Just for that, you'll make me hop around, eh?"

SUNNY (smiling): "Then why did you punch me yesterday, even though I said bats" and they chuckle at his attempts to heckle her.

MAITRI (suggesting): "Why don't you all play hopscotch with me instead." They grimace at the very feeling.

SUNNY (responding): "We'd rather do something more boyish like have *scotch* instead" and the boys gleam at the thought.

MAITRI: "Oh God. Don't you all have anything better to do at this age than taking to drinking?"

HARRY: "Don't worry. They're only teasing you. We do have our collection of stamps, marbles, comics and sticker games that we exchange."

MAITRI (relaxed): "That seems to be more like us trading in dolls and related stuff" as the boys chuckle away to that.

As they grew a bit older into their secondary section, it was Tushar who started becoming friendlier – he made more friends than the others. Sunny started picking up things faster than the others. As for Harry, he would always be engrossed in his own toys. Maitri, on the other hand, would take in everything that was being taught and also what wasn't being! Participating in sports was a completely different story, with Harry doing well in athletics and Maitri being good at badminton.

MAITRI to Tushar (imposingly): "You will HAVE to take part in the physical education drills. They have made it mandatory for every student." Tushar is taken by surprise.

TUSHAR: "Okay. Sunny, you too will need to participate in the school drills."

SUNNY (nonchalantly): "I'm not going to torture myself" Everyone stares at him in disbelief.

TUSHAR (seriously): "But they will penalize you in your academics if you don't."

SUNNY (angrily): "What the f**k. I don't want to grow up and become a Milkha Singh" They all laugh at his typical reaction.

After the drills, **SUNNY** said to Tushar (exhaustedly): "I'm just SO drained out – I think I'm going to die" as they all stare away towards him.

TUSHAR (smilingly): "C'mon, *yaar* (dear). It can't be that bad. I don't believe that for a minute" and everybody shook their heads disbelievingly.

HARRY: "It'll make you healthier, Sunny."

SUNNY (suspiciously): "By the way Tushar, who told you that it was compulsory?" and they all look at each other smiling away.

TUSHAR (chuckling): "Maitri" as he suddenly begins to feel warmer, only to realize that she's glaring away angrily at him.

SUNNY walked up to Maitri and said (exasperatedly): "Why the hell did you put me through this? Now they're after my life to take part in the drill, 'cause they think I'm interested!" And they all laugh out loud at that.

MAITRI (reasoning): "So what's the problem? Simply tell them that you aren't" and everyone around smiled.

SUNNY: "Do you seriously think that I haven't already? Still, they've been chasing me like a parent."

MAITRI (smiling): "So good *na* (right)? You certainly look like you could do with some activity." They all cackle louder to that.

SUNNY (realizing): "Oh! Now I get it. You purposely put me through all this, haven't you?" The rest of our friends exchange high-fives.

MAITRI (justifying): "C'mon. You will get fitter with all this."

The others all nod at this comment.

SUNNY: "We're not shoes or clothes that need to fit."

HARRY: "Well – I really see nothing wrong with it."

SUNNY: "You NEVER see anything at all – so where's the question of right or wrong?"

HARRY is visibly upset by his friends comment and our friends guffaw at that remark.

(Casually) "Maitri – you should be playing games that are right up your alley."

MAITRI (curiously): "Such as?"

SUNNY: "Volleyball. With all your verbal volleys, you would've been good at it

Sunny and Tushar laugh away.

MAITRI: "Very funny – dear *Sunny!*"

TUSHAR: "You guys are downright hilarious. You really should try your hand at Squash, as you'll squash out all your differences neatly"

Sunny and Tushar continue to laugh at their own jokes.

SUNNY (appreciating): "Good one, mate!!"

The climate changed a bit and they all caught *fever*. Don't worry. We've all caught it at this particular time of the year. It's called the examinations fever. Our friends are all hitched up together to do some serious group studies at one of their pads...

SUNNY (fed up): "I'm going out of my mind with all this studying!" All of them agreed.

MAITRI (reasoning): "That's exactly what you need to do – get all other matters outta your mind" and they laugh at that.

TUSHAR (sarcastically): "Huh? Till all our grey cells fall out, is that supposed to be it?"

He looked at Maitri who was looking extremely glum and looking for clarifications. .

HARRY (seriously): "No. What she means is all the other distracting stuff."

Maitri now nods in agreement.

SUNNY: "And empty our minds?? Don't you know – an empty mind is a devil's workshop."

MAITRI: "How will it remain empty? Won't it get filled up with all the cramming?"

Of course, everybody agrees to that.

SUNNY: "When do we fill the glass with water? When we want to drink it, right?"

HARRY: "Well, yes. But what if we don't want to get up at night to fill it?"

MAITRI (casually): "Knock it off, Harry. Knowing Sunny, he'd raid someone else's stock." They all agree vehemently to that.

SUNNY: "Hey – I'm not that bad. I'd head out to fill it after I've emptied it (from my body)." Some of them laugh at the implications.

HARRY: "If that is the case, then why study all the year round?"

TUSHAR (resignedly): "Don't take it so seriously. Que sera, sera (What will be, will be)."

They all accept that, as it is a fact that we cannot completely control what happens in our lives.

The exams done and dusted, they returned to their regular classes. Following was the narrative in their class before one of those periods...

"Welcome ladies and gentlemen, boys and girls. We now have a wrestling match coming up. Harry and Tushar are slugging it out over who will treat the other. We have the support coming in from Maitri and Sunny – who will also join in for the grub. The match has started with punches landing randomly on each other and blows are being exchanged; of course everyone is egging them on. More than wrestlers, they look like Messi – what with their *messy* hairdos and crumpled clothes. It seems the one who is at a vantage position when the teacher walks in will be declared the winner by the majority present here. In the beginning, it was Tushar who managed to stay on top but later on, it seems that it is Harry who is *harrying* him. They keep trading positions while the crowd's composure changes from delight to despair with every turn they face. Suddenly, the time-up alarm sounds and the winner is ... Tushar who manages to snatch victory from the jaws of defeat by pulling at his clothes. Everybody rushes to their place with the slugfest participants taking up the back benches. The takeaways include a stiff shoulder for Tushar and a sore eye for Harry. Life goes on in the class as they hide behind the front benches to catch their breath, wits and composure. With this we bring you to the end of the live coverage. It

THIS USED TO BE MY PLAYGROUND

was a very exciting match and I hope you enjoyed every moment of it."

Later on, our friends start chatting away in the school canteen during one of their breaks...

MAITRI (warmly): "I just adore Science for all the nature that it stands for. Guys, each of you tell me which your favourite subject is?" They all look at her strangely.

TUSHAR (chuckling): "Then you must surely be getting a lot of *nature calls*." Tushar's comment is followed by peals of laughter all over.

MAITRI (justifying): "I would rather put it like actor Jim Carrey does in his Hollywood movie Ace Ventura about wildlife." Now it is everybody's turn to be impressed.

SUNNY (smugly): "You would definitely need cages to store all the kinds of organisms, a whole lot of fresheners to counter the odor given out by various substances and a lot of chains to tie down your equipment before they take off in your zoo."

Soon they all are in splits imagining the scene so vividly described by Sunny.

TUSHAR: "I for one love all the varied locations that Geography teaches us about. I would like to visit them all sometime."

MAITRI: "YIKES. I hate it for all that stuff about the countries, their locations, their resources and the likes. It's so damn drab" Most of them agree with Maitri's reasoning as she continues... "Also, are these places we talk about peculiar only to a country or are they found

19

across the globe?"

TUSHAR: "But I'm sure each and every place is unique in its own way. No place on this earth can be duplicated – especially by name. Perhaps the climate and conditions could be similar and even the name can be similar sounding, leading to confusion."

MAITRI: "Oh really? Then where the hell is Petersburg – Australia, Russia, USA, Canada or Germany?"

TUSHAR: "Shucks. You got me there. I see what you mean. You're absolutely bang on about all of those countries having a city by that name, except the last one. That's Petersberg and it's in Germany. By the way, how did you know about all this? Is it just a passing interest or are you getting fond of it too?"

MAITRI (snidely): "I was searching for something and just so happened to discover this by chance but hey - you're so right about the fact that it really sucks. But that's not the only instance of duplication of its kind in the world. Even London exists in UK as well as SA, as does Georgia" and now his friends look approvingly towards her and disapprovingly towards him.

TUSHAR: "I'm really stumped. Since we're on the subject, another interesting trivia on duplication is that of a country and state both share the same name, viz. Georgia. While the former is caught between Europe and Asia, the latter is in the USA."

HARRY: "Let me see. Mine is definitely Maths for topics like *Derivatives*, Componendo, Dividendo, etc."

Maitri (animatedly): "I *comprehendo* – my dear *friendo.*"

SUNNY: "My favourite is similar to yours Harry – that game *Nintendo*" They all chuckle at the reference.

HARRY: "Tushar – you should also take a crack at it."

TUSHAR: "Ok. I really think you can use *Derivatives* to make some good money in the market."

SUNNY (eagerly): "Any other favorite Maths topics, Harry?"

HARRY: "Well – I also love the Parabola and Hyperbola formulae"

Now its everyone's turn to appear flummoxed.

SUNNY (chuckling): "Ahem – while this isn't a parable, it has all the making of a *hyperbole*"

All the friends are at a collective loss for words.

TUSHAR (intrigued): "Parabola or Hyperbola, *yeh kya bola* (what did you say), *kyu bola* (why was it said)" and they all burst out laughing, whilst nodding their heads in total approval.

HARRY (joining in): "Maitri, your favourite subject should've been Maths, as your favourite topic has just got to be *Sy-maitri* (Symmetry)" Once again everybody laughed away to that.

MAITRI (Gesticulating towards Sunny and Tushar): "Your subjects should've been *Moral* Science, as you could definitely do with some *moral* policing."

SUNNY: "But as our morale is very high, we can do

without that. Besides, I have all the moral support that I would require – coming from Tushar right here" while the both of them exchange high-fives with a smiling Harry and forlorn Maitri looking on.

MAITRI observes Sunny and Tushar cowering over, whispering something and guffawing away looking towards her, to which she questions them "What is it? Please share it with us too."

The friends are all ears (and eyes too).

TUSHAR (straightening up): "Sorry Maitri. I can't share this one with you!" He can't contain himself and bursts out laughing along with Sunny.

MAITRI: "Oh c'mon – I can take a joke or two. I can guess that it's a girlie joke" Soon everyone forces them to share it.

SUNNY (cautiously): "I'm sure you're familiar with *mensuration* too due to the menstruation cycle..." Suddenly the group is shocked at his crudeness.

HARRY (sensing Maitri's discomfort tries to change the topic): "BTW – which is YOUR favorite Sunny?" He manages to successfully divert them.

SUNNY (pensively): "That would certainly have to be History – what with all the evolution of races and its epic battles." Our friends are definitely perplexed with his choice.

HARRY (disgustedly): "Ugh. That's too confusing. It's like the chicken and egg story – which Mughal sultan invaded first and which one ruled first..." They all vociferously agree.

TUSHAR: "Yikes. How can you like learning all about how our parliamentarians manage the show – in Civics – they themselves have no civic sense, driving around in a Honda Civic." They all burst out laughing.

HARRY: "Sunny, I've just got to warn you here to be very careful or you may have to repeat the class."

SUNNY: "What are you saying? I've never been a failure yet and have no real intensions of beginning now."

HARRY: "Haven't you heard the adage that '*History always repeats itself*'? That sure would imply that you'll flunk or should I say *duck*, coz you're taking to History like a duck takes to water" They all shake their heads in disgust at that remark.

MAITRI: "Shit. All of us like different subjects!" Her friends all seem to realize this fact only after she says it.

HARRY: "Dunno about you guys, but I have a lot of trouble remembering names. Hence, I like it when the teachers come up with mnemonics like this one for our eastern and southern States in Geography "Three sisters – Tripura, Megha, Asha had a friend Aruna who saw a *Naag* (snake) with a Mani (pearl). They blurted out *Hey Ram* (O Lord), let's take the BOAT." The sisters and their journey cover the eastern parts of India – namely Tripura, Meghalaya, Assam, Arunachal Pradesh, Nagaland, Manipur, Mizoram while their vehicle covers Bengal, Orissa, Andhra Pradesh and Tamil Nadu." Tushar is apparently amused.

TUSHAR (excitedly): "Maitri, there's one for you too in Biology "Kings Play Chess on Fine Glass Sets." This stands for the animal classification system hierarchy from Kingdom, Phylum, Class, Order, Family, Genus to Species." Maitri is visibly surprised.

MAITRI (animatedly): "Just you wait, Harry. There's one for you too in Maths "King Henry Died; Mother Didn't cry much." This covers the entire distance hierarchy namely kilometre, hectometre, decametre, metre, decimetre, centimetre and millimetre." It is now Harry's turn to be amused.

SUNNY: "That's enough of mugging up. At this rate, we'll only be remembered as complete *muggers.*"

TUSHAR (guffawing): "Now be careful. Too many of them mnemonics might give us a strong bout of *Pneumonia*" They all cackle away to that the silly joke.

SUNNY (putting it to rest): "That's not necessarily true. All of us most certainly do like 1 subject a lot– namely ICT" to which they all blurt out in unison an emphatic "YYEESS."

Soon our friends had to submit one of their high school assignments. Sunny who was nominated as the leader by them, allots the work that he gets to his team...

He says to Maitri authoritatively: "You find out how important trade is to commerce" She listens attentively and readily agrees to comply as it is the joint effort that is ultimately going to achieve results in this case.

MAITRI: "Done. I'll work on both of them."

SUNNY: "W'okay."

Next, he walks up to Tushar who seems to be wearing a long, puzzled look on his face and tells him rather arrogantly: "You take care of the winds of change."

TUSHAR perplexedly: "Okay… fine" when actually it wasn't and Sunny starts to stare at him.

Both of them get busy with their respective assignments, but they observed that Sunny himself was not occupied with any of the work as such…

TUSHAR (curiously): "Hey Maitri, I haven't seen Sunny working on ANYTHING for this project, have you?" Maitri too suddenly realizes that.

MAITRI (agreeing): "That's what even I'm thinking! He always seems to be free."

(Excitedly) "Let's catch up on him!"

And they proceed towards him stealthily…

TUSHAR: "Hey Sunny, wassup bro?"

SUNNY: "Hey – you guys finished with all your stuff so soon?" Tushar and Maitri look at each other.

MAITRI: "First tell us – what is the part that you're doing in all of this?" Tushar backs her up looking questioningly at him.

SUNNY: "My work begins where yours ends."

TUSHAR: "How's that possible?" and even Maitri scratches her head in amazement.

SUNNY (stone-faced): "See, it's like this. I will collate your completed matter and add the images" They both seem to be satisfied with his justification.

Convinced, they proceed to complete their work and submit it to him in a couple of days. Now, Sunny approaches Harry and says (casually):

"Hey bro, you need to work on this assignment – Trade Winds" Harry is in rapt attention.

HARRY (validating): "Which part of it?" Sunny begins to look away contemptuously at him.

SUNNY (firmly): "All of it" and Harry is pretty confused at that.

HARRY: "And what about you'll?" Sunny looks him square in the eye.

SUNNY: "We're all working on our individual topics. He snarled. So, now get on with it" as Harry too decides to go along with his brief.

Harry, as was his wont, proceeded to step on it. He worked hard, completed it quickly and in a couple of days handed it over to Sunny. At submission time, the teacher started calling out and discussing every team's project in class while Maitri, Tushar and Harry started to look out for both their leads as well as project to be called...

MAITRI (anxiously): "She's still hasn't called out ours" and they all nod in agreement.

TUSHAR: "And she's almost done too!"

HARRY (visibly upset): "Exactly. Come to think of it –

where's Sunny's, by the way?" while now his friends realize that he's nowhere to be seen.

TUSHAR: "He was supposed to have consolidated and submitted both Maitri's and my topics." Harry's astonished to hear that.

HARRY: "Oh is it? And the topics were?" as his friends are confused whether it is his query or doubt.

TUSHAR (blurting out): "Mine is 'The Winds of Change' and Maitri's is 'The Significance of Trade Winds to Commerce" Harry is all messed up on knowing that they're all working on the same thing but before he could say something –

The teacher called out the topic 'Trade Winds'…

MAITRI (mumbling): "Hey Tushar – that sounds like a medley of our topics."

HARRY (blaring out): "Hold your horses! This is MY topic" as he proceeded to raise his finger and submit his topic on his own – looking around but still not able to find Sunny anywhere.

Maitri and Tushar now began to realize that this was their combined original topic. They inform Harry later on that he had just submitted their group topic and that too working all by himself while they in turn worked on a dud project.

HARRY (pensively): "Guys – come to think of it – we've been had. While Tushar's supposed topic is actually a track on a path breaking event – an English song called 'Winds of Change' from the epic rock band Scorpions,

Maitri's supposedly is about trade and Sunny's – well – his is 'zilch', 'nulla' – meaning nothing except twiddling thumbs!"

This realization between the 3 of them soon turned to anger when it dawned on them that they had all been short-changed by him.

Thus enlightened – after the class – they all belted out in unison "SUNYYY!!!"

They fought and made up, faced ups and downs and yet bonded together – all the while having a lot of fun.

Soon, an excursion known here as a field trip came up. At first, some of the parents were reluctant but when they learnt that it was mandatory and their kids were hell bent on it, they gave in.

This was one *assembly* they all loved, as it gave them a lot of time to have fun. Their buses started for the camping destination and our friends had a lot of fun along the way till they reached.

Our dear friend Sunny thought it will be all fun and games but how wrong he was proved – right from the time they reached their destination. Throughout the trip, all of them had to keep attending to some or the other explanation on the village they'd visited. After all – it was supposed to be an educational trip. Gradually, even Tushar started getting jaded on having to collect artifacts of the place which they would require to submit as part of their project. Maitri, though, loved it and Harry even enjoyed it. They even volunteered to help the villages in their daily chores and won them over. Sunny and Tushar– thought they had gone back to stone ages and were sorely missing civilization. They kept muttering "We want to go back to the future." While the former trio welcomed the rustic environment, people and the food, our latter pair was missing their new age surroundings. Sunny felt that their school had taken the *field* trip a little too seriously and sent them out in the field like cattle to graze! Tushar felt that they were being trained to be servants – what with all the helping and assistance!

Finally, after what seemed like an eternity to some, the 3-day trip came to a close and everyone started packing up. Our dear friend's faces lit up with the prospect of heading back to familiar *lairs*. Meanwhile, the weather turned moist with all the emotions, as few of them started bidding goodbye to the gracious villagers. They all started back for their school and made a lot of ruckus on the way. They all reached their respective homes to their parents, who were relieved to see them back safe but not *sound* – as they had lost something on the way. No – it wasn't their mind or their senses; it was their voices.

Needless to say, Sunny and Tushar goofed up big time in the assignments. This came as no surprise – given the extent of their participation.

During their school vacations, our friends really started freaking out. They would follow their schedules with such punctuality that wasn't seen even in their school timetables! Initially, they went all comical - gorging on fictional comics…

TUSHAR (vigorously): "Maitri, give me Phantom" as she reluctantly gives in.

MAITRI (excitedly): "But then in return I want Tin-tin" and now it's Tushar's turn to hesitate.

TUSHAR: "Thank God you didn't ask me for this *Phantom* (cigarette candy) 'cause I wouldn't have given it anyways."

MAITRI: "And why not?"

TUSHAR: "Coz girls don't smoke."

MAITRI (upset): "Oh c'mon. But these are for everyone."

SUNNY: "Yeah, just like the *buddhi ka baal* (old lady's hair) – better known all over as candy floss" while the boys roared away that – much to her dismay.

HARRY (anxiously): "Sunny, pass me Mandrake" to a frowning Sunny.

SUNNY (exasperatedly): "First give me Superman" as Harry repulses at the thought. Soon, they would complete their favorite books and exchange them for other publications. Their rapid-reading *rapidly* exhausted their monthly library memberships within a week.

To divert their creative energies during the day, at first, they started turning their attention to indoor board games like Snakes and Ladders, Ludo (a token-based one), Housie (bingo), Chess, Carom, Business (Monopoly), Spell-o-Fun (Scrabble) etc. Ludo, though, wouldn't be any less sinister than Chess, though it also did favor survival of the quickest or should we say the fast and furious. They even played card games like Uno, Bluff, Donkey (an elimination one) as well as Antakshari (a Bollywood singing one). They would imitate grown-ups – be it playing homes complete with various member stereotypes, enacting shops scenarios and banks – counting cash vigorously with virtually anything deemed as currency, office, play doctors using multiple things as examination or even surgery props, behave like bus conductors and ticket examiners – each of them performing their roles like seasoned artists. (Pity that their own children would have to go to play zones and pay exorbitant prices with real money to play these very games at children educational zones like Kidzania). These, of course, were interspersed with some outdoor games like badminton, tossing the Frisbee, Dog and the Bone, *Lagori* (an object-based running one), *Kho-Kho* (a push-based running one) and hide-and-seek. At times, the guys had extravagant choices to play many boyish games like cricket, football and even marbles while the girlies largely were very poor with limited choices playing only games like hopscotch. (Maybe that's why men guzzle scotch more than women – to make up for the lost years! Maybe women too play more mind games for the same reason!). Soon they diverted their energies to more gender-neutral games like throwing the ring (trying to win objects around which it settles) and creating paper boats in a pond.

With the vacations ending, this gaming bug only grew bigger when they all started playing X and 0, Join-the-

Dots, Hangman, etc. and the guys even played Book Cricket during free periods and compulsory attendance periods right after their exams. Circulation took on a completely new meaning for them as they even exchanged their comic/books with other classmates. And their choices changed as they would now squabble over some local interesting Indian stories like Tinkle, Jataka Tales, etc. (Their kids would be busier than them even without playing a fraction of the games)

As they grew older, they took to the legendary adventure books like Hardy Boys – for the boys, of course and Nancy Drew for the gal. As their liking for this genre strengthened, the four of them started devouring the series – slugging it out for their copy. Needless to say, they had a roaring time devouring these famous publications and had whetted all the local libraries...

HARRY (puzzled): "Does this library move?"

SUNNY: "Should it? Are you sick?"

HARRY (astonished): "NO. I mean does it rotate, revolve or move around in circles – whatever else it's called?" They all give him a strange look.

TUSHAR: "This isn't Mumbai's famous Ambassador Hotel. For God's sake, it's a freaking library" amidst shushed reactions all round.

MAITRI: "What's wrong with you?" and they all looked curiously at him.

HARRY (softly): "Then why is it called a circulating library?" They all burst out laughing and continued laughing even as the quartet was put out of circulation from the library that day.

That didn't stop their mischievous ways, as they continued their adventures by chewing gum, blowing bubbles as well as the gum at passers-by, startling them. Soon, they turned to TV, lapping up the evergreen comedy series Laurel and Hardy and Charlie Chaplin

With the new age, their choices too underwent changes as now they were all hooked onto Archie comics. They could relate their situations to those depicted in these comic books collectively. As usual, they would have frequent spats in order to get hold of the copy. Gradually, the guys switched to indoor games of a different kind – TV video games like Nintendo, Atari and Play Station. (They didn't know it as yet but their children would play some of the board games on their phones! But they couldn't do the mischief of cheating by dropping their friend's coins or even flicking some play money, just to get ahead). The outdoor games remained just that – outdoors. Games became sports as they merely began watching them on TV instead – including cricket, tennis, racing, etc. while the gals got busy exploring and experimenting with their own looks and fashion. At night, they all would turn their gaze towards TV programs and got hooked onto stellar shows – be it sci-fi ones like Star Trek and Fireball XL5, as well as bonded over other shows like Different Strokes, Wonder Years, Dougie Houser M.D. and the hugely popular F.r.i.e.n.d.s.

As their vacations got filled up, they started grudgingly

gearing up for grind coming up ahead.

Our friends were going through identity crises – when they had to select the subjects for higher education. While for some it was a calculated decision (counting the subjects), few selected by playing the elimination game *Akkad bakkad bambe bo* (Eeny Meeny Miny Moe – the English game) while others took a very deliberating decision – they deliberately chose the easiest of subjects! Well – so much for future planning and the likes. Everybody wanted to stay away from heavyweight subjects that required a lot of preparation and effort...

Soon, like all good things must come to an end, it was time for all the fun and games to stop. Time started running out on our friends, as they started approaching matriculation completion...

SUNNY (tiredly): "Phew, finally, our bored exams are nearing! After that we'll be out of this jail" They all smiled at the intended pun.

TUSHAR (eagerly): "Before that, I'm really looking forward to the farewell" This time, they all nodded excitedly.

HARRY: "Really – it's more important to fare well in our exams."

MAITRI: "I too want to complete my Grand Slam book."

HARRY: "Bah, make that my SLAM book."

TUSHAR: "Umm, of course, you mean the *Grand Slammer*, pardner – as in bridge or even in baseball." They smirk away at the analogy – nodding their heads in approval.

MAITRI: "Right now, all of you'll fit nicely into a nice big Slammer."

TUSHAR (seriously): "Well – I don't know about this slamming business but I do hope that it will be a grand farewell."

SUNNY (butting in): "Hey guys, why all this bookish stuff? Haven't we had enough of books to last us a lifetime? Can't we stay in touch and meet up? Your farewell preparations look more like a *final goodbye* or better yet an *obituary*. Lighten up guys" This made them all burst out laughing.

TUSHAR: "But it's quite possible we'll get caught up in our lives and won't all be able to meet up regularly again…" and suddenly they dread that indeed that was a distinct possibility or worse yet could even become a reality.

MAITRI (grimacing): "Yeah. And all these great times might remain just that – memories!" Our friends become morose at the thought.

SUNNY (countering): "Come on guys, in these days of technology, there's no one who can't be reached – nor any limit to the memories that can be created to go with the existing ones…" Everyone cheered up a little with that thought.

HARRY (reasoning): "True. But what if we don't respond – being busy in our lives?" Obviously, he felt that this was a possibility.

SUNNY: "I'm sure all of us will, except for THIS girl here."

MAITRI: "With your high flying life, I'm willing to bet, if any one of us don't make it, most definitely it's gonna be you. I, for one, wouldn't ever leave this group, come what may" while his friends now start to look contemptuously towards him.

TUSHAR: "I too will be accessible." They were happy to hear that.

HARRY: "I three."

SUNNY: "Amen...plus two more –."

MAITRI (interrupting): "And A Woman!" and they all cheer on to that.

With that sentiment, they return home amidst collective contagious bonhomie.

HARRY (pensively): "After watching that childhood video, I was just introspecting a few days back on my progress." Our friends all looked towards him.

SUNNY: "That's called 'reminiscing' bro and I must confess I've just been bitten by that bug too – after watching that."

TUSHAR: "Yeah. It's certainly contagious, as I too am recollecting our fond memories."

MAITRI: "I remember how you guys used to wager on which school bus would reach first."

SUNNY: "I vividly remember how I used to relish having cheat snack sessions right through the class" as they all look towards Sanaa who lights up to the very thought of it.

MAITRI: "You were always tongue-in-cheek whenever you spoke but actually your *tongue was never in your cheek,* even when you were silent – as you were busy eating." The friends all burst out laughing.

TUSHAR: "Hey guys, we've never heard your memories. C'mon – share some incidents" and he gesticulates towards the others.

SUNNY (pondering): "I used to make a lot of paper rockets and *launch* them at unsuspecting people who would find them *landing* on their heads or worse yet target their noses or ears."

MAITRI: "As for me, I would make friends with that chip-chop thing (a folded-paper tool for making friends) that would help us pick common interests by color, number, etc."

HARRY: "I would make people *threadbare* by catching their hand in that thread game" The guys chuckle away at those girlie games.

MAITRI: "HEY, didn't we both relish irritating people by splashing rain water on them, wearing gumboots" They all visualized merrily how they frolicked about in the collected water.

TUSHAR: "Remember how we used to fight over how not to enact the dumb charades names."

SUNNY: "No wonder those years are called the wonder years!"

HARRY: "I think it's more to do with us *wondering* our

way around."

TUSHAR (sniggering): "I recollect once I had asked my father to get me speakers with more music clarity, as I was and still am very fond of music. He promised me ones that I won't even be able to see from afar, at one go. I started having gleeful visions of a multi-part speaker system. Imagine my plight when I saw what he got for me – a headset!"

MAITRI: "One of my other favorite subjects used to be Art and Craft. I used to love how we would make those fancy paper objects" and everyone gives her a harried look.

TUSHAR (mockingly): "You must've been very crafty in all your dealings!" She gives him a stern look and the others smile.

SUNNY: "*Witchcraft* is more like it."

MAITRI: "Yum. That certainly reminds me of Kraft cheese along with those famous other French brands."

HARRY: "You must've been good in handicrafts. You've been a more than handy student as well as always had an avid interest in craft items" as she's embarrassed at that compliment while some of them begin to mock at his honesty.

TUSHAR: "Maitri sure is handy at throwing whatever she can lay her hands on, at me – having given me a couple of handicaps."

SUNNY: "Maitri, is your aim that poor? I could help improve it."

TUSHAR: "No. You didn't get it. She's good but I'm a better dodger" and he exchanges high-fives with his best pal Sunny.

HARRY (captivatedly): "Maitri, you've always been the one mesmerizing us with your magical hocus-pocus at studying. No wonder you've reached these dizzying grades."

SUNNY: "Make that a treacherous bit of 'Hokey-Pokey'" and she's alarmed by that remark while the rest of them smile.

MAITRI: "I'd rather groove – following the steps – of the famous song by the same name."

SUNNY: "Why, come to think of it, I'd rather down the ice-cream of the same name" while that moves everyone to get into the mood for some and they proceed to order it.

MAITRI (firing a salvo): "You're more suited to the hanky-panky instead."

SUNNY (retorting): "Why you! Person of double-standards! Did you'll notice the deception at work – turning it back to me swiftly?" Everyone laughs away merrily to that.

MAITRI: "How does that make me a person with double standards?"

SUNNY (sniggering): "You're a double stickler for standards – remember making me do the drills just because the teacher said so and also for liking two subjects" and all our friends are in splits at that remark – including the person in question.

MAITRI (countering): "If I'm a person with double standards, then you're a person who's double the trouble – just like that famous classical Hollywood movie 'Double Trouble'."

HARRY: "He sure eats double, so I guess you can also add that famous Hollywood movie 'Double Jeopardy' to his labels."

SUNNY (turning on her): "Where's the science to that title here on the eating, miss 'Scientific'?"

MAITRI: "You see, you used to smell like a chemistry lab once you'd be done with your assignments. I should know – majoring in Chemistry" and everyone howls away to that reasoning – some even shuddering, remembering those days and the stenches they brought along, leaving him red faced.

TUSHAR: "Oh yes. I had completely forgotten that our party-man here is also a 'farty-man'."

MAITRI: "And you-know-what? He was all of 16 at that time!"

SUNNY (enthusiastically): "Reminds me of that wonderful riddle of the 3 huts and why the villager wouldn't go to hut no. 17 from amongst 16, 17 and 18. Do you'll remember or should I give the answer for your benefit?" while everyone is at a loss trying to recollect it.

(Continuing): "Here it goes…"

"Firstly, you've got to write the numbers in digital style and then shift the page upside down. Then NO17 can be read as LION which is why he wouldn't go to that hut" and our friends can't stop laughing – clutching their tummies to that.

TUSHAR (animatedly): "Here's another similar 1 – an update to that digital 7. A lady walks into a garage and asks a mechanic to give her a part – part no. 710 which she lost from her car. When a puzzled mechanic questions her, it turns out that it was OIL written on the lid of the engine oil container which she read upside down as that no."

HARRY: "We've also moved up in TV programs from 'What's the good word?' to 'Whose line is it anyway?'" and everyone smiles away at the realization of the metamorphosis being conveyed – starting from a word and ending with a sentence.

SUNNY: "I don't know what we'd really do without the all-important supplement sheets that we die for in the dying minutes of our exam papers.

TUSHAR: "Speaking of supplements, our very own soon-to-be Silicon Valley is full of just that – silicone" and the guys chuckle away naughtily to that.

MAITRI (suspiciously): "What for?" as that leaves them all tongue-tied.

TUSHAR: "Wafer chips for computers" he says sheepishly while suddenly breathing heavily.

SUNNY (defending): "They're silly little cones – hence

called silly-cone" and they all laugh nervously while Maitri buys it.

MAITRI: "What would you call a person who always doles out complements?" as they're all at a loss for words.

(Answering): "We call such a person a 'compliment-ary' person!"

HARRY (pensively): "All this frequent travelling reminds me of the English song 'When It's Night-time in Italy, It's Wednesday over here' from the Everly Brothers" that elucidates the peculiarities, cultures and time-zones of various global places" while everyone's awestruck at his memory.

SUNNY: "Little Miss intelligent, pray tell me why our family names are only called sir-name (surname) and not madam-name?" They all laugh away at that look of helplessness on her.

That said, they completed their paranoia over the nostalgia and turned their sights to their upcoming college lives. After struggling for the last couple of months before their exams, they were finally free to live their lives according to their choice …

And soon they all got engrossed in their final exams. How time flies! Their exams were over before they even realized it and they become free birds after that. Vacation too came and went like a breeze and before they knew it, they got their convocation decree and the much awaited college time had finally arrived! Their results were out. All of them applied for Computer Engineering to the newly formed College of Information Technology (CoIT) and promptly also got through. They were fortunate enough to be together in this lovely stage of their lives too...

SUNNY (proudly) "We'll all become Bachelors of Engineering – once we graduate."

TUSHAR (smilingly): "Really" he said amidst total laughter.

HARRY: "Finally, we're on track to become somewhat like a certain Mr. Gates!" Everyone's looked star struck.

MAITRI (looking starry eyed): "Oh yeah!" and they all started dreaming of making it big.

Suddenly Sunny started crooning a famous classic Hindi song from the Bollywood movie *Albela:*

"*Bholi surat dile ke khote* (Honest face evil intentioned)

Naam bade aur darsaan chote (Big reputations but small presence)" as they all look at him in amazement at the rendition.

TUSHAR (puzzled): "How so?" as everybody began fathoming the relevance.

SUNNY (reasoning): "You see – he started with gates but ended up with only windows" and they burst out laughing at that.

TUSHAR: "Good one. Now that you've mentioned that movie *Albela,* I'll give you another one..."

And he starts crooning an old Hindi song from another

Bollywood movie *Kabhie Haan Kabhie Naa…*

"Woh to hai Albela (He certainly is different)

… *Sadaa tumne aib dekha, hunar ko na dekha* (You've always looked at his weaknesses, never looked at his capabilities)" as everyone hums along but fails to understand the reference.

MAITRI: "Now who's that supposed to be?"

HARRY (explaining): "A certain Mr. Jobs is the complete opposite. You see – though he started off with a job but still landed up creating an entire empire – Apple" as they all laugh loudly.

SUNNY (arguing): "But the former has created a bigger corporate empire – Microsoft" and some of them rallied round his contention.

MAITRI (trying to pacify the situation): "Easy does it boys. Now don't go start those software duels all over again. We've got many more where they came from." sensing that they would have another of their fights over choice of technology to deliver solutions.

And college life continued with their usual bonding and banding.

2

BLOSSOMING MUSHROOMS

Our friends started meeting more frequently. They would hang out together more often; be it while attending college or outside it or even at their other haunts. A-ha, some new people have joined our dear friends. Meet the *tall* Lynda; out-thinking her was a tall order – literally! Here's Sanaa, an average looker. Out-talking her was even more difficult, as she's anything but silent! Next up, there's Manprit or Manu – the handsome angry young man who would get into a fit of rage in a jiffy at the smallest of things. Soon they became a team and together, they took many sojourns. Life became a beach party. They all became models! While our Maitri had turned beautiful and slim, Tushar was now a very handsome guy, Sunny a strong decent looker and Harry – a Mills and Boon stereotype of TDH (Tall Dark Handsome). All the latest fads would be aped. Every day was no less than a fashion parade. Slowly, stylists and makeover consultants started opening outlets near the newest fashion hub. Fashions would soon change faster than seasons did! They all started idol worshipping celebrities in their idle state. Cultures, mannerisms, tastes, interests were inspired from the westerners.

As they started coming of age, Manprit started developing fondness for Maitri. Slowly, our hot man turned in hot pursuit of his muse. After countless requests and gifts, he finally managed to get her attention and *affection*. Soon, they started spending more and more time with each other. Once, they got so close in class that the professor had to literally separate them i.e. make them sit separately. Don't let your imagination run wild. For the love birds, this was no less than a separation – akin the main leads in the Bollywood movie *Veer Zara*! While Manprit began pining for his love in his newly imposed exile, Maitri longed to be united with her *subject*! Finally, their ordeal ended and they were united again as the lecture ended. Wait – their romance doesn't stop here. They resumed their rendezvous in various cinema halls and even theatres. While they would enjoy every show together – their theatrics sometimes kept the other viewers more entertained than the main show itself. "CUT (IT)!" some enterprising people would yell out sometimes – laughing away, as though they were shooting, making them realise that they wanted them to stop! They started becoming famous in cinema halls as

Ramu and Jhulan (taking after the famous duo of Romeo and Juliet) with the ushers and cleaners alike politely informing them…

"*Saheb, show khatam ho gaya* (Sir, the show has completed)" as everybody around would chuckle away.

Soon, the guys took a liking to the romances depicted by the celebrated novelist James Hadley Chase and the gals to Mills and Boon respectively. They would read them with avid interest to the love lives portrayed…

MAITRI (inquisitively): "Hey – aren't you guys reading about that Brit secret service spy agent '007'?" The guys all smiled.

TUSHAR (giggling away): "No. That's from Ian Fleming. This is a generic suspense thriller" Maitri is embarrassed at this while they all had a hearty laugh.

LYNDA (admiringly): "Wow. You guys are real bookies" while they all look at each other chuckling away to a rather astonished Lynda.

SUNNY: "Though we're not really betting bookmakers, you can still bet on us" They all howl at the joke.

LYNDA (exasperatedly): "Should I say book*worms* instead?"

MAITRI: "Now don't go about opening a can of worms with just your *bookish* knowledge" and they roar away at Maitri's attempted swipe against Lynda's jibe.

HARRY (pacifying): "Chill – guys. Take it in good jest" while they all rally around.

Slowly, they started dabbling a bit in Information Technology – incidentally, the actual reason they were here anyways!

TUSHAR (profoundly): "Hey, actually the software goes into the hardware" as they all nod their heads in approval.

SUNNY (amusedly): "And to think that the seniors kept telling us that it's the hardware that has to be inserted" and everyone burst out laughing at that remark.

LYNDA: "I know. Anyways, this hardware business is actually too hard to digest" and they all nod in agreement.

SANNA: "Yeah. Even this software is a bitter pill to swallow, better yet than the former."

MAITRI: "I guess folks – this is *IT*!"

HARRY (appreciatively): "Way to go, Maitri." They all seemed impressed by her wit.

Look what have we here... two foodies biting away at each other! For Sunny and Sanaa, it seemed like it was love at first bite! They had hit it off instantly. Slurp! They would be found in each other's arms munching away. Even their favorite English song was a lilting stunner called 'Love Bites' from the rock band Def Leppard. They were so fond of foodstuff that both would write blogs and – unknown to each other at that time – subscribe to each other's blogs. Imagine the look on their faces when they finally met up in person. It became a mutual admiration society! Like true critics, they would always be found trying out different dishes at various places – sampling each other's dishes for their respective blogs. After all, work comes first and food was their passion (at least the first passion anyway!). They behaved so identically that people used to mistake them for siblings – what with their relishing each and every dish. They would even gulp down the same way, giving the same expressions and even the same sounds (comments, burps and farts included). They soon became the resident food experts, whom their friends would look up to for guidance – especially those who felt badgered at eateries with those big names for the dishes in those gigantic menus! Why, our friends here could pass any foodie exam with flying colors. They would even win those all-you-can-eat contests comfortably and were always infamous at such places as *Kheer and Ganja,* instead of famous Hindi folklore romantic couple *Heer and Ranjha.*

TUSHAR (smiling): "Guys, I even remember her favorite poem – Georgie Porgie Pudding and Pie…" as she gushes away in embarrassment.

SUNNY (amusedly): "I'm proud of you for this, Maitri" and they all laugh away.

MAITRI: "And which was your fancied poem, Sunny?"

SUNNY: "Oranges and Lemons" while now it was Maitri's turn to feel elated with that, as the rest of them just shook their heads – laughing.

MAITRI (smilingly): "That figures. And yours – Tushar – most certainly must be *Goldilocks* – what with that long mane of hair that you put on your shoulder" and they all howl away.

Soon they learnt about the D word everyone dreaded. No, it wasn't the D gang, it was Documentation...

MANPRIT (exasperated): "Oh God! So there's still much work that we'll have to do over and above the software creation" as they all shook their heads in pain.

HARRY (reasoning): "Yeah buddy. We need to pen our plans for it to *pan* out the way it was designed but don't worry – you'll be part of a team of people working on it. After all, as Sunny says, 'Rome wasn't built in a day'" and everybody stares at him in disbelief.

MANPRIT: "I know but spare a thought for the hard labor – just like those workers that built *Rome*."

HARRY: "Life isn't all fun and games. You know – we have to work too."

MANPRIT: "Bro – not documentation. Yucks! I don't want to become a *writer*" as everyone guffawed.

HARRY (arguing): "But you'll become an artist one day. After all – writing software is also like a drawing – a piece of art. It's a creative job" while they like the sound of that and seem pleased with the thought.

MANPRIT (sarcastically): "I don't know about that but the lord sure has created a *work of art* with you" and everybody smiles at that.

HARRY (upset): "That wasn't funny."

MANPRIT: "Cause I ain't *Sunny*."

HARRY: "That wasn't either!" as they all realize how easily Harry is offended with that remark – like always.

MAITRI (calmly): "Chill – guys!" while they restrain him from starting another fight.

The case of our other friends namely Harry, Lynda and Tushar was the typical old triangle. You see – all had an affinity for Geometry. But there was a small twist in the tale – we just couldn't figure out who was *tailing* whom! Tushar and Harry were always good buddies. Lynda would see this bromance regularly. Imagine her surprise when they would chase her by turns – even though both of them liked her. Somewhere along, she started feeling like a rationed commodity like in the olden Quota-*raj* (state regulation) days and was shocked with the bonhomie between the two. They looked more like Siamese twins when they would try to woo her turn by turn. At times, Lynda would start feeling as though she's playing a dice game like Ludo and found it all too dicey. They had so much respect and understanding for each other that she herself started getting confused between the two. She would get all mixed up with whom she

IT'S NOT ONLY LOVE...

went where during her narrations – amidst the hilarious laughs of the twins. They started getting famous in a very different way. "Awesome" is what Lynda heard people say to which our guys started laughing away. On further prodding them – to her dismay – she discovered that those people were actually saying *Threesome!*

Soon they began learning what software standards *stand* for …

TUSHAR (exasperated): "With all this standardization, I feel as though I work for the ISI" as they all chuckled.

SUNNY (whispering): "Sshh, be very careful of what you say! Don't ever disclose your identity. Even the walls have ears" and they all wore a puzzled look – looking at him.

LYNDA: "Come again?"

SUNNY: "Don't you see – you will be deported" while they still couldn't make neither head nor tail of it all.

SANAA: "For standardizing things?"

SUNNY (explaining): "No re (Not at all). For being a spy" while now they got the point he was making.

TUSHAR (gesturing towards Lynda): "Like how you would call that James Bond Hollywood movie (softly) A spy who (was) loved (by) me" and they all look on approvingly.

LYNDA: Get real, buddy."

TUSHAR (clarifying): "Sunny – ISI is our very own

Indian Standards Institute – the ISI marked products, not our neighbouring country's spy agency Inter-Services Intelligence ISI" while everybody snickers away.

Whichever college picnics they went for, their reputations preceded them. While Romeo's and Juliet's romance gained prominence, our troika wasn't far behind, as were Kheer and Ganja. Old friends would meet up in such get-togethers but would always get confused between friends and partners. Maitri's and Manprit's love blossomed; Sunny's and Sanaa's mushrooms bloomed while Harry's, Lynda's and Tushar's *pakti khichdi* (cooking rice-cum-lentils) even turned to *biryani* (cooked rice-cum-vegetables). Gradually, their parents got wind of what was cooking behind the scenes, as they all began to spend more and more time in each other's company together and separately.

Soon they started learning a new language for software development. Java it was.

TUSHAR (poetically):

"Mar java, mit java (Will die, will get destroyed),

Tere iskh mein paagal ho javaan. (Will become insane in your love)"as they were all impressed at his ongoing efforts to propose to her.

LYNDA (amused): "How very filmy, you *flimsy* Tushar!" and they all laugh at her repartee.

SUNNY: "If this is what they speak in that country (Java), next up will they also teach *Sumatra*?" Everyone chuckles to that.

MANPRIT: "I just love the Java constructs and the structures, as I'm fond of *curves*!" The men smile away but the women don't take too kindly to that remark.

MAITRI: "Shut your trap, Manprit" but the gents still continue to grin away.

HARRY (musingly): "Those *Pointers* are so groovy" and the guys cackle away – much to the disapproving gazes of their partners.

MAITRI: "Anymore of your nonsense and I'll just kill you'll!"

MANPRIT (smiling): "Seriously. I also adore databases – as I love bases" while the guys sigh away strongly.

MAITRI (reasoning): "Oh, is that so? Then you should've further pursued *Chemistry* where you would've got compounds too to go with them" as now the girls laugh away at the speechless guys.

Amidst all the fun, they had finally managed to complete learning the entire software engineering lifecycle...

LYNDA (exhaustedly): "Phew. This looks like Darwin's theory of evolution!" as they were fed up of all the learning.

TUSHAR (adding): "It's more like a revolution, coz my

head's dizzy with all that stuff revolving around in it." Everyone smiles at that.

MAITRI: "What an analogy, Sunny!" and they seemed to agree to that.

TUSHAR: "But why did it have to be that of a butterfly? It would've been better if it'd been that of us humans."

LYNDA (reasoning): "Don't you see – it's so much easier and direct – like from the apes. Rather than from the larva to the pupa to the cocoon and finally to the stage when they develop wings" as everyone wore a very jaded look.

MANPRIT: "I don't want to be a pupil anymore. I've got enough *pupils* to see well enough!" And everybody laughs their heads off to that.

SUNNY: "Continue speaking about the wings, especially if they're chicken's" while his and Sanaa's mouths starts watering at the very mention of that word.

SANAA (nodding): "Yum" and everyone shrug their shoulders resignedly at them.

TUSHAR (animatedly): "Lynda, why don't you just stay put in that cocoon of yours since you love it so much" as his friends all snicker away at his snide remark to her.

LYNDA (chuckling away): "Why yes – you baboon. As you say. From now on, I will stay put in it – just to be away from you" and they all have a nice laugh at the cat and dog fight.

Now well – what've we here? Looks like a prospective lovers' tiff! It did seem that love is in the air and that love makes the world go round and all that mushy-mushy – no mushroom though – unfortunately for our foodies. Fortunately, it's sorted out and things are ok. Soon, the software that's known to drive people nuts seemed to have started working on our friends too...

SANAA (grinning): "Arithmetic Logical Unit (ALU) reminds me of a Hindi song from the Bollywood movie Mr. and Mrs. *Khiladi*... "

"Jab tak rahega samose mein ALU (Till the time a samosa contains potato) –"

MANPRIT (jutting in): "*Sunny rahega oh tera bhALU* (Sunny will remain your bear)" Everyone laughs vigorously – holding on to their tummies.

SUNNY: "I'm proud of you, Sanaa."

MANPRIT: "Likewise when I hear of Random Access Memory (RAM), I go...

"Hare RAM(a), Hare Krishna, ... (Dear Rama, dear Krishna)" and they all sway away, chanting the *enchanting* hymn.

HARRY (resignedly): "*Hey RAM* (Oh my god)" as everybody laughs out to that.

Once they were hanging out together and the gals realized that the guys were discussing something animatedly...

TUSHAR (softly): "… checkout… …." as the gals look at each other – astonished at their brazenness.

LYNDA (grimacing): "Stop it guys. You're being creepy" and the guys stiffen.

MANPRIT: "What gives?"

LYNDA: "You think we're all fools here? We know you'll were ogling and commenting at the girls passing by – you ogres."

TUSHAR: "It's not what you think it is; in fact it's what you don't think it is"

MAITRI: "Huh – wazzat supposed to be?"

TUSHAR: "You see, we're just discussing our next holiday plans and when to checkout of the hotel" while the guys heave out a huge sigh of relief.

MAITRI: "Oh c'mon. We even heard you discussing sizes with cups and what-not" and the guys were dismayed to discover they had overheard them clearly.

SUNNY (straight-facedly): "We were discussing how much the bill comes to per plate – hence the cups reference."

SANAA: "Yeah-yeah-yeah. And you guys expect us to believe that trash that you've *dished* out?" The gals laugh at them.

MANPRIT (to Maitri): "Easy does it – my dear buttercup.'

MAITRI: "Knock it off. I want no buttering up."

SANAA: "You should take a leaf out of the organization

People for Ethical Treatment of Animals (PETA) who protest against being selective about body parts."

TUSHAR (fondly): "I should surely like to take out the leaves, as well as, *take-out* the very campaigner too." The guys suddenly start grinning again with the gals appalled at their open defiance.

LYNDA (resignedly): "Sheesh, they're referring to that leaf-covered campaign by that famous American model Pamela Anderson" and the gals start squirming in discomfort at their corniness.

Another time, the gals witnessed Tushar being a bit hesitant with both Sunny and Manprit trying their level best to coax him. They swiftly joined them to understand what the dilemma was all about...

SUNNY (explaining): "You have to ask her out else you'll remain one of her admirers forever." Everybody nods their heads vigorously in approval.

MAITRI (smiling): "Sure. She would definitely ask you to go out" and the gals laugh away at having stifled his solemn advice.

SUNNY: "Well – you have to ask her if you really want to date her."

SANAA: "Your advice is certainly very outdated."

SUNNY (exasperatedly): "I give up. You know what's to be done, Tushar" while the guys appear jaded and the gals freak out at their expressions.

It was time for our friends to *gradually* graduate. They worked out, *literally*, on their assignments or projects – as it's called – in the industry. Soon, their assessments were complete and they were not only awarded their certificates but they were also provided placements in some of the well-known software companies. Payday with the *Peddhe* (sweets) started for them as finally, they began to stand on their own two feet – it was no mean feat, both financially and emotionally!

3

PAYBACK TIME

Our friends now had settled into some of the IT companies. Sunny, Lynda, Tushar and Sanaa all got through as trainees to the services behemoth Software Technologies (ST). While Sunny, Lynda and Tushar joined a software team, Sanaa worked in the sales team. Maitri and Manprit joined the IT division of International Travels Information Technology Systems (ITS) as trainees. Both joined the development team. Harry got through at Services Systems (SS). He joined the programming team as a trainee. All were happy to have landed up jobs upfront. They were however a trifle disappointed that they couldn't be together anymore.

They all soon met up after 3 months to exchange their immediate feelings...

TUSHAR (rather elated): "Hey guys. We're glad to have made it to ST!" Everyone's in a jovial mood.

SUNNY (relieved): "Yep. We have finally cracked it after all those interviews. I was beginning to feel like some celebrity" and everybody laughs away.

LYNDA: "That's true. With all the tests and paper work it looked like a mini-project in itself."

HARRY: "What are you'll cribbing for? Guys, you'll have all the luck. Firstly, in ST, that too together, a good package – what else could you ask for?"

SUNNY (reasoning): "Well – for starters, that's not entirely true. Sanaa doesn't work with us. Secondly, we're bonded laborers (signed a bond) for two years. You, my dear friend, are a free bird!" while the ST mates sighed.

HARRY (chuckling): "But one who can only fly within the confines of a small room" as they laugh at the analogy.

MAITRI (reasoning): "At least you're not caged! We're placed under house arrest with these in-house projects" and the others look puzzled.

MANPRIT: "You're not even constrained. We have our certificates handed over to ITS, as though we're some kind of a university – issuing them certifications!"

HARRY: "Lynda, you'll also get free training. And Maitri, you'll have something that we all don't have – job security in the EDP department."

SANAA: "We have fewer chances of promotion, though."

MAITRI: "You'll get to do more things and learn more"

while the others agreed.

TUSHAR: "You'll have lesser controls and procedures – which means more freedom."

MANPRIT: "Now who needs to stop cribbing?" as people listen in attentively.

LYNDA (yelling): "HEY people. Let's leave out all this heady stuff. Each has its own pros and cons. It's been a long time. So, let's catch up, instead" as they all agree to that.

All was forgotten soon, as they had a lot of fun.

Soon, they began to get busier and busier...

Maitri and Manprit were soon joined in their team virtually by Farooq – a freelance tester. Although they couldn't meet him, they had a video conference with him. He was average looking and casually dressed all the time. Soon, they started getting engrossed in their projects. However, they got fed up when Farooq started keeping them hanging on long hours for his test report. When they reported this to the management, they worked out a solution where Farooq would come in for a few hours every few days of the week – as and when required.

Once, in sheer frustration, **MANPRIT** started crooning a Hindi song from the Bollywood movie *Ilzaam:*

"I'm a freelancer(I'm a freelancer),

(chorus)

aata hu, jaata hu (I come, I go)

rato ko, logo ki, neende churata hu (At night, I steal people's sleep)" as everyone is in splits at that rendition.

MAITRI (reasoning): "You've got the moves and that's supposed to be street dancer – not freelancer. Interesting adaptation, though"

He stated emphatically, though...

MANPRIT: *"Agar koi kide nikle, to Ilzaam Farooq pe hi lagna chahiye* (If you find any bugs, blame Farooq for it)" and they all hada hearty laugh.

MAITRI (approvingly): "*Ise kehte hai nehle pe dehla* (This is called one-upmanship).

I'm proud of you, my dear" while everyone claps away to that.

Harry directly reported to his boss. Well, directly, because the boss was the owner. Harry would thus be able to do as he pleased. He would perform all the functions of software engineering. He began to see himself as a one-man army who would handle everything with his boss being just a figurehead – busy in the business. He realized that in a small setup, everyone performs multiple roles. How prophetic Maitri and Tushar's words had turned out to be. He also began seeing himself as a Project Manager. As work increased at a faster pace, the owner decided to rope in a consultant, Chirag, to manage the project. He was very authoritative and extremely polished in his appearance, so much so that Harry thought to himself "Yuk. It looks like he's put on some vessel shining polish like *Shineit* – as makeup – which makes him look so shiny. I think he should be called *Shiny*" and he laughs silently at his own thoughts. He thought that Chirag looked more like a very expensive doctor who we would just consult for a few minutes and send the client away. Initially, Harry took it in his stride, as he realized that he hadn't really managed a team as yet and needed to gain experience as a Project Leader first. He began expecting a small team where he would eventually lead. Though time started passing, the team never came. Soon, he began hearing about Chirag's loose ends – not shoring up the standards and worse yet – not following established engineering procedures. He began losing respect for Chirag. He started speaking his heart out to Parag – the peon...

HARRY (exclaiming): "Parag – why even you're more valuable to SS than that Chirag," as Parag is startled out of his wits.

PARAG (surprised): "What are you saying? He's a consultant and I (am) only a peon –" Harry gags him.

HARRY: "... who doesn't play his *part*."

PARAG: "Really?"

HARRY (amusedly): "Absolutely. At least you're taking care of the office, helping the boss in banking work, paper work, getting refreshments for us..." Parag feels very happy about all the compliments that he receives.

PARAG (opening up): "Frankly, I really love it. Before you joined (us), I would get bored and sleep all day." Harry's extremely surprised to hear this.

HARRY (curiously): "Is it?" as Parag went on to explain.

PARAG: "Yes. And (the) boss used to (try to) do everything himself. When I told him, I could help him (with some of the things), initially he was hesitant but I'm glad he finally listened (to me)!"

HARRY: "See – your English (language) too is good." Parag gleams at that fake compliment.

PARAG (countering): "Boss has helped (mould) me to become a better worker." Harry is actually happy to see him progress.

Harry now began teasing Chirag by calling him *Parag*. Initially, Chirag thought he said it accidental. Once, the boss walked in on one of the incidents. Since he had been getting reports of irregularities from the clients, he straightaway knew Harry was the one who was troubled and so he had begun checking up on Chirag. Ultimately, he decided to do away with Chirag and hired a couple of programmers – promoting Harry to the position of a developer – much to his relief.

Meanwhile at ST, Sunny, Lynda and Tushar were joined in their team by a web designer Avis and an analyst Davis. While the former was almost good looking and a wee bit plump, the latter had rugged looks. Sanaa, too, had a mixed bag of other sales professionals for company – some dashing while others heartless.

TUSHAR (amusedly): "Sanaa, now you can talk to your heart's content. Nobody will ever stop you!" They all laugh away.

SANAA (remarking): "Very Funny! You'll are a big team. You people will have lots of fun" and they all begin to realize that she's actually very jealous of their strength.

LYNDA (reasoning): "And lots of work too" as the rest looked at her sympathetically – but not too *pathetically*!

As they started functioning as a team, they discovered the virtues and pitfalls of specialization...

SUNNY (anxiously): "Oh God! I'll now have to segregate development and design" as that set them all worrying.

LYNDA (justifying): "Of course. This is not your project. You'll have to section-ize your work" and everyone starting thinking away.

TUSHAR: "If you look at it differently, it enables you to focus only on the programming."

SUNNY: "But I used to fulfill my artistic streak that way."

LYNDA: "Now, you will have to implement whatever it is that Avis comes up with."

AVIS: "Yeah bro. I'm sure you haven't yet used the latest designing tools

SUNNY: "Well of course not! Who do you think I am – a

graphic artist?"

AVIS: "There's more to my work than just design. I also create animations." Everybody is quite surprised to know about that.

LYNDA (amused): "Oh. So, you're more like a painter – creating a piece of art!" They all look admiringly at Avis.

DAVIS (adding): "And guys, I'll provide you with the specs" and now they turn in his direction.

TUSHAR: "We don't need them. Maybe you can't see very well but we all can, right guys?"

DAVIS: "I'm only referring to the specifications for development, not the spectacle that you make of yourself."

LYNDA: "Oh, so you mean the requirements gathering stage of software engineering."

TUSHAR: "So he'll make *documentaries*" while they all laugh away to that.

SUNNY: "Avis, I guess now you will completely design the system – since you're a designer. That will leave us all with twiddling thumbs."

AVIS (sullenly): "I haven't freed you'll up just for nothing. You'll have to assist in updating the documents in the process that you're a part of."

TUSHAR: "But who will design the data structures, now that Manprit isn't with us?"

DAVIS (watching the others giggling away): "What's so funny? Was he the database analyst?"

SUNNY: "Nothing, pal. It's just our private little joke."

AVIS (continuing): "We'll have Database Analysts (DBA) and Quality Assurance (QA) resources from other departments performing their respective functions and the system design being created by an Architect" while everybody listens in keenly.

LYNDA (explaining): "You see, the software creation process is very similar in certain respects to the construction process – what with both having Project Managers and Architects, the former's building a foundation to the latter's plinth, the first one's creating layers to the second one's slabs, the former's data access routines to the latter's plumbing and electrical wiring, the first one's delivery to the second one's possession."

SUNNY (bowing): "Point taken milady – from the learned Lynda!" as they all start banging away on the table in appreciation.

Slowly, their frequency of meeting started diminishing – they met once in a month...

HARRY (gesticulating): "Hey guys, how's it going?"

TUSHAR (responding): "Well, their romance is going really strong – despite the separation."

HARRY: "Wha - whose and what separation?"

TUSHAR: "Sunny and Sanaa. They are staying apart; in different departments" as our friends fumble trying to stop themselves from laughing out loudly.

SANAA (furiously): "That isn't funny at all."

HARRY: "And work?"

TUSHAR: "I guess – a lot of coordination required – what with working with so many people from so many departments" as they all agreed.

SUNNY: "And you'll, Manprit?"

MANPRIT: "Well – we have a lot of work pressure with the users taking us for granted!"

LYNDA: "How so?"

MAITRI (explaining): "Well, they don't collate requirements. They give them one-by-one knowing that we're around, resulting in our support prolonging by more hours."

SUNNY (reasoning): "At least you'll are together in it. Your company is called ITS and it's obvious that for you'll, it's only love" as everyone let out a pining sigh.

SANAA (smilingly): "And what about you, Harry?"

HARRY: "Life's been good. You're no longer speaking to a trainee!" and they all begin to congratulate him.

MAITRI: "So this party is on you now, eh?"

HARRY: "Hold your horses. My pay is still a constraint and I won't be able to sponsor this party. However, who knows – with an increment – maybe a smaller party – in the near future." Everyone lets out a sigh of disappointment.

TUSHAR (questioningly): "And, I suppose you M's must be with each other all the time?"

MANPRIT: "No. We're also separated by the users of different departments" and they all laugh away to that situation.

TUSHAR: "What kind of a boss do you have, Harry?"

HARRY (smilingly): "Well, mine's a real Time Master, more like that hit character Crime Master Go-Go from the Bollywood movie *Andaz Apna Apna*. He forces me to keep track of how much time I spend on everything in a blessed time 'shit'" as they all howl away.

LYNDA: "But at least it helps to record our work done – especially for future reference – when we tend not to recollect clearly."

HARRY (asking): "And yours, Sunny?"

SUNNY: "Well – we had a potentially nasty face-off with him."

MANPRIT (curiously): "Is it?"

SUNNY (excitedly): "You see – he's really nasty and he overheard me calling him a snake when we were talking about him in our team!" as everyone listen in attentively.

MAITRI (eagerly): "Oh no. And...?"

SUNNY: "I convinced him that we were discussing the hit English movie Snake in Monkey's shadow. Phew!"

LYNDA: "Trust Sunny to come out of any situation unscathed!" as they all try to take advantage of the opportunity and start patting his shoulder real hard while he tries to out-maneuver them.

MANPRIT (anxiously): "Harry – at least you only have to

worry about time. Here, our boss thinks this is a circus. He's the ringmaster with the hunter and we're all the animals whom he lashes out to. The users are the clowns of the show – what with their funny clothes and funnier faces" and everybody laugh away hilariously at that depiction.

Life passed by as they got increasingly involved with their work. There was always more and more of it. One day, Tushar was sitting in a corner grinning away vigorously...

LYNDA (perplexed): "What are you laughing at? Please share the joke" as everyone hearing this gather in.

TUSHAR: "I feel as if we're on a school trip, as we have a *steering* committee to drive our project just like a bus!" And they cackle all away.

SUNNY (animatedly): "And we travel by the escalator to escalate the issues. Why, we are even issued a *ticket*!" That brings out all round laughter.

MANPRIT (pointedly): "The *principal* consultant thinks that he's a school principal. He himself has no *principles* – to speak of..." And they all guffaw away.

TUSHAR: "For all the mess that he has created, we should execute the senior executive."

MANPRIT (closing up): "And all the stakeholders could just become skate holders and just skate away from this dull meeting like some cheapskates who've made it just for the free grub on offer" and they all grin from ear-to-ear.

By now, our dear friends had gathered some real creditable experience while at work. They soon started comparing notes...

SUNNY (admiringly): "Sanaa, I must say you have acquired some good soft skills."

SANAA (spurning his advances): "I know where you're headed. Don't you ever dare hit on me so hard with your soft approach!"

DAVIS: "Easy-easy, guys. Looks like you all have started your grub talks again."

MANPRIT: "No buster, for once they're not talking food here!"

SUNNY (amorously): "I agree. While we've got busier, they've gotten *busty* and even gone *bustier*."

MAITRI (picking up their bags): "What say Sanaa, let's bust them up!"

SANAA: "Yeah. They've gotten outta hand."

Needless to say, the guys were pricked with *needles* by the ladies!

4

RISE AND SHINE

With all this work, our friends would always be at their wits end. By now, they found different ways and means to cope up with the pressure in the late evening hours…

avis, dancing to the famous classic English song from pop artist Glenn Frey:

"… The heat is on …" as their friends start swinging.

DAVIS (swaying away): "No maan. You should be singing this classic English song from the legendary pop artist Billy Ocean 'when the going gets tough, the tough gets going'" while that really sets them moving.

TUSHAR: "Oh c'mon. To get my mojo going, I can't do without a light."

SANAA: "And I with some serious caffeine!"

DAVIS: "I agree. I too need tea as a small recharge to charge myself up."

LYNDA (disapprovingly): "That's just not right guys. At least music is a bit better. After all, we want a temporary diversion, not a permanent distraction" she says amidst a lot of booing.

SUNNY: "What say guys, isn't this the very trait that separates the mature from the immature" while they all give him a big glare while she smiles.

AVIS: "No Sunny. We need to refresh ourselves to find a solution to our technical problems that we get stuck in often. And as it is – immature actually consists of the words 'I'm mature'" as they exchange high-fives at that response.

TUSHAR (supporting): "Yeah man. Seriously! And you Sunny – you get those power breaks when you remove all the crap – that's in your mind – from your body in the toilet." Everyone laughs loudly at this.

LYNDA (smilingly): "That's a load of *shit*, literally!" she says, amidst even more guffaws.

SUNNY(retorting): "Why yes, come to think of it, even Manprit takes 40 winks in any ramshackle department on his way about the users."

TUSHAR: "How can you be sure he wakes up after exactly 40, not more?" Once again it got them all grinning at that.

SANAA: "Exactly. Each person has a different way to get

their creative juices *flowing*, much like water from a tap."

LYNDA (a repartee): "Guys, thanks to the internet, you can get every solution you're searching for online."

AVIS: "I beg to differ. My problems are so unique that only I can resolve them."

SUNNY (smiling): "Well – a yes and a no. We do discover solutions but then again, at times, we don't" and there are mixed signals from them.

Slowly work increased even more and there was no time left for them to unwind at the office at all…

TUSHAR (anxiously): "Guys, its 9 o'clock already and we're still here working away!" They all look away exasperatedly.

LYNDA (calmly): "Yes. And it looks like the hour digit has dropped over from 6. Still some way to go, though" They smile at her analogy.

SANAA (eyes lighting up): "Let's order a working dinner to save time" while suddenly everybody starts to give it a thought.

TUSHAR (figuring out): "Well guys, we should stop by 11 to try and make the last train."

SUNNY (relaxed): "Don't worry. We'll get reimbursed for the leisurely travel, if we're to miss that."

LYNDA: "But we'll be subjected to intense grilling from

our parents for the time."

SANAA: "No such problems here."

LYNDA: "Really! How so?" as they begin to wonder.

TUSHAR: "Guys, don't you know – they've MOVED."

LYNDA: "Somewhere close by?" as now her friends began to laugh at her ignorance.

TUSHAR(laughingly): "Yeah. Really-really close!"

LYNDA: "WHERE???" while she restlessly awaits the answer.

TUSHAR: "Into each other's arms (gesticulating)" while her friends began to hoot away.

LYNDA: "Oh wow – is it? Now I get the drift. So howz it been going?" They begin to shake their eyebrows in eagerness.

SANAA (blushing): "Well, so far so good" as her friends call out 'oh-oh'.

LYNDA: "Last I knew you'll were on PG but wasn't in on you having moved in."

SUNNY: "It's more practical – the need of the hour" while the men nod vigorously in approval.

TUSHAR: "Not to mention convenience" as the men now blurt out 'hmm'.

SANAA (wizening up): "Shut up, Tushar!"

LYNDA: "So, no nagging, only *necking* and more" as our people utter a rather big 'OH HO!'

SANAA (embarrassed): "Please, guys!"

TUSHAR (opportunistically): "As you say. Let's all join the honeymooning couple and have some fun."

SUNNY (graciously): "But of course. You'll are always welcome guys."

TUSHAR: "Sunny, no wonder I see you nowadays all in red and pink and not black and blue."

SUNNY: "*Kuchbhi* (Anything?). Nobody would dare beat me black and blue. Lest you forget, I'm a guy and can never be *red* and *pink.*"

TUSHAR: "A domesticated one at that. He's no longer a *bachelor* in a bachelor pad."

SUNNY: "Well, I'm not married just yet."

TUSHAR (teasingly): "That's a mere technicality. Are you telling me you aren't in a relationship and free to play the field?"

SUNNY (looking dreadfully towards Sanaa): "*Marwaega kya* (Do you want to get me killed)?"

TUSHAR: "*Ghar gurahasti seekhega* (You'll learn household chores)" as everybody bursts out laughing.

SUNNY (sighing): "You're telling me. It's not all *hunky* dory."

TUSHAR (curiously): "Not even for a hunk like you? You mean there's trouble in paradise?" as everybody's in splits.

SUNNY: "Lots. There are problems within and outside

the house."

TUSHAR: "It can't really be THAT bad, huh?"

SUNNY: "Really. Can't finish all the chores as both are tied up and then there's pressure from our housing society as well."

TUSHAR (smilingly): "Well, you can address the latter by making a commitment" while they all nod away in approval.

SUNNY (dejectedly):"*Pagal hai kya* (Are you nuts)? As an adaptation of that famous dialog from the Bollywood movie Wanted, he went...

Ek bar jo maine commitment kardi (Once I've made a commitment),

To mera khud ka baap bhi meri nahi sunega, (even my own dad won't listen to me),

Leave alone hers" as everyone guffaws away.

LYNDA (worriedly): "So, next step?"

SANAA: "We're evaluating and will let you'll know whether it's really worth it at all" and Tushar is flummoxed with the timing though he expected her to jut in.

LYNDA (changing the topic): "What's with Maitri and Manprit?"

SUNNY: "Theirs is the usual office romance."

TUSHAR: "But won't they get closer?"

SUNNY: "Well, theirs is work in progress (WIP) with all

that mushy stuff."

TUSHAR (laughingly): "If theirs is a WIP, when will yours be *finished goods*?" he said amidst laughter all over.

SANAA (offended): "Ouch. That's an awfully nasty thing to say!"

SUNNY: "Our foodstuffs are our children" as people nod resignedly.

TUSHAR: "But don't they get in the way?"

SANAA: "NO."

TUSHAR (seriously): "Well, your denials can't hide the cold hard truth that you'll are both having affairs outside your relationship with your foodstuffs" as everybody chuckles away.

LYNDA (laughing): "The passion fruit has literally remained just that. It hasn't *ripened* and so we have *unfulfilled* passion."

SANAA: "Et tu Lynda (You too, Linda)?"

TUSHAR (clapping): "Bravo Lynda! What a parting kick. You would've made those famous free-kick *footballers* like the British David Beckham or even Brazilian Roberto Carlos proud!"

Soon, they were all nearing completion of their probation period…

TUSHAR (surprised): "Oh God. It's review time."

MANPRIT (grimacing): "Nightmare time, actually" as they all laugh away.

SUNNY: "All this nervousness from the tension makes me feel as though my churning stomach has become some kind of a fish-pond. Hence, I need some good fish to add to it."

HARRY: "It's a low tide now, dude. You won't catch any good ones."

(Continuing) "Also, that pond is way too big for any small fry" he added, confusing one and all.

SUNNY: "Whoa?"

Harry (reasoning): "You see – when you're in a big pond, you're a small fish."

SANAA: "Wow. I'm amazed at that analogy!"

MANPRIT (deducting): "Going by that, Harry, you're a big fish."

HARRY (arrogantly): "Yeah. Size matters. It enables me to do more, grow faster. Besides, I have virtually no competition in my space, nay my territory."

TUSHAR (taking pot-shots): "Make that your *Terrortory*" he said amidst peals of laughter.

LYNDA: "Harry, you might be doing more but we're definitely learning more."

SUNNY: "True. With all the structured systems, processes and scale, we gain bigger experience–."

HARRY (interrupting):

"*Agar jal mein rehna aai* (If you have to stay in the waters),

To jalki rani banke rehna (then live like the queen of the waters)."

MAITRI: "Scale brings with it latest equipment, state of the art facilities."

HARRY: "It collectively helps the group but hampers the individual rise."

SUNNY: "This healthy competition teaches you to be like global companies, not like our old businesses protected by archival laws that makes paper tigers out of all."

TUSHAR (admiringly): "Well put, Sunny."

They were all in a foul mood when they met up next, after their appraisals had just completed…

TUSHAR (disappointed): "There's nothing creamy about the *incre(a)ment* that we got." All our friends sneered.

SUNNY (animatedly): "I swear. What *KRAzzy* KRA (Key Responsibility Areas)" and they all smile away to that.

HARRY: "Good one, Sunny!"

LYNDA: "Seriously. We weren't even given an opportunity to have a say in it."

SUNNY (pouring his heart out): "We're made to feel guilty for all the work that we put in and none of its good enough!" Everybody nods in approval.

MANPRIT (calmly): "Relax guys. It can't be that bad."

TUSHAR: "Easy for you to say as, you all are all a cost centre, unlike a profit and loss one like us."

SUNNY: *"I'm increasingly incensed by the insensitively inclement increment."* He says amidst a thunderous applause and their *tongues* get all twisted trying out that impromptu tongue-twister.

LYNDA: "Wow. Adversity brings out the hidden poet in you. Well put, Sunny!"

MAITRI: "I've always been *wary* of this variable pay business."

TUSHAR (seconding): "That's right. How can people like us from operations, unlike our mates from sales, have a salary component that's dependent on the company business?"

SANAA: "Well – as the saying goes – everyone's a sales person!" And they all jeer away at the comment.

TUSHAR: "If you overkill, then you'll create a situation similar to the famous play 'Death of a Salesman' from the celebrated writer Arthur Miller."

MANPRIT (satirically): "If you take a blood test, your blood group will now show up as S. Sales is now circulating in your blood."

SANAA: "Very funny, Manprit!" she says mockingly.

HARRY (adding): "Sanaa, don't ever donate blood. You will convert the recipient into a hardcore sales professional!" There were peals of laughter all round.

TUSHAR (rubbing it in): "People in your vicinity will have to watch out for mosquito bites, else even their blood groups might change" and our friends start joining in.

SUNNY (announcing): "Vampires beware. Don't bite her!"

SANAA: "Calm down guys. Else you'll get arbitrary sales targets too!" Everybody suddenly quietened up at that possibility.

HARRY: "But good that none of us are trainees anymore..." Everybody nodded in approval.

LYNDA: "Well, we could have also become seniors."

MANPRIT (countering): "It's difficult to move from a trainee to a senior directly."

LYNDA: "But it's not impossible, especially if you have learnt and done a lot."

HARRY (cutting in): "Btw guys, I'm thoroughly pleased to announce that I've been promoted to the rank of a team leader." Now the lot had something to cheer for.

All of them (together in a crescendo): "CONGRATS! WE WANT (A) PARTY-PARTY-PARTY."

Harry started crooning a Hindi song from the Bollywood movie *Bajrangi Bhaijaan*

"*Aaj ki party meri taraf se!* (Today's party is on my behalf)" and everybody dances along.

SUNNY (as the crescendo softens): "Harry, *acha hai ki tumne woh Aladin ka Chirag pochkarke jinn se manga ki wo khud gayab ho jaye* (Harry, good that you wiped the Aladdin's lamp and wished for the lamp itself [Chirag] to disappear).

Tabhi to tumhara rasta saaf ho gaya (That's why your route got cleared)" while they all burst out laughing.

After the initial ruckus, they calmed down. A few days later, our ST mates suddenly saw Harry in their office...

TUSHAR (amazed): "What a pleasant surprise! Guys look who we have here!" They are surprised to see him walk up to them.

SUNNY (introducing him to Avis and Davis): "Guys, this is our dear school-cum college mate – Harry" They shook hands.

Avis and davis (collectively): "Hello Harry."

SUNNY (introducing them to Harry): "These are our twins and partners in crime – meet Avis and Davis. You got an example right now itself" and everyone smiles away.

HARRY: "Hmm. Not only do they sound like twins, they also look identical. What's more, had they been standing any closer, I would've mistaken them for conjoined twins!" Everybody laughed and continued to laugh even more on noticing that both Avis and Davis are laughing away in synchronicity.

LYNDA: "So sweet of you to drop by to meet us, Harry."

HARRY: "I haven't just dropped in; I'll be staying back. You see – I've been hired by your company for the project."

TUSHAR: "That's wonderful news!"

SUNNY (wisely): "Oh, now I see why SS gave you a double promotion – in order to push you through to companies like ours."

LYNDA: "Point. One thing though – now where did that fish logic of yours go, Harry."

HARRY (smiling): "*Nowhere*, its right here. Being a big fish has enabled me to jump into this bigger pond. Had I been smaller, I wouldn't have been able to make it here.' They all smile at that retort.

LYNDA (refuting): "While that may be true, on moving, you have become smaller as the pond has become bigger." Now our friends sensed an argument coming up.

HARRY (contesting): "You're missing the point. Though this definitely is a bigger pond, I'm still a bigger fish than you all." Everyone is shocked at his insinuation.

TUSHAR: "HOW can you even afford to say that?"

HARRY: "I'm here only because I'm a big fish. They already have many smaller fish…" Our friends now start getting a bit upset with Harry's new found attitude.

SUNNY: "What is the logic behind that claim of yours?"

HARRY: "Since they have many other smaller fish, they brought a bigger one instead to show-off their acquisition for something like an aquarium. It's nice to have all kinds." Harry's words begin to sort of agitate them all now

TUSHAR (arguing): "But how can you put different species together?"

HARRY: "Well – there are some that can survive with the others."

SUNNY: "And then there are some that won't be allowed to…" as Harry looks stony-eyed at that threat.

LYNDA: "Guys, let it rest. This will never end. At least we're all confirmed. Let's live and let live."

TUSHAR (backing her up): "Both of you start singing the cult English song '*Live and Let die*' from the rock band Guns 'N' Roses" as Harry belts out the lyrics – with Sunny joining in and Tushar. The others were utterly astonished at how instantly and effectively, music killed their differences.

Our dear friends now began working more closely. After a few months, they met outdoors again…

MAITRI (happily): "Wow. Nice to hear that Harry has joined you'll at ST" as the rest nod away joyfully.

MANPRIT (ecstatic): "Yeah. I had a lot of fun. How have you guys been finding this sudden development?" and they are all curious to know.

SUNNY: "Lovely" as his ST mates seconded.

HARRY: "The other day, I saw Manprit and Maitri making out – er – something" while this causes some of them to gulp down their sips.

SUNNY (in *splits*): "You mean they were brazenly making out in public?"

MANPRIT: "What rubbish. What he means is that he saw me *taking* her out, so we were *hanging* out and he had trouble *making* that out" as everyone guffaws away – shaking their heads in disbelief at the situation.

(Continuing while gesturing towards Harry): "And how has it been going for you?" Everybody looks at him, eagerly awaiting his response.

HARRY: "Exciting, I'm really enjoying being with them."

"I feel like James Bond, the secret agent, on a mission – except that there's no secret about what I do."

TUSHAR (seriously): "There is. The *cigarette* (secret) is there *na* (right)" as everybody burst out laughing.

SUNNY: "Harry, SS is a body shopper and it's your body that they've sold to ST. Hence the origin of the term 'body shopping'."

HARRY (upset): "Hey, you're making me out to be some kind of a prostitute and SS to be like some kind of pimp!" This is surrounded by even more snickering.

SUNNY (smilingly): "At least I'm not making SS out into a morgue" while our friends now just couldn't stop laughing.

TUSHAR: "And what's your take on the women, Mr. Bond? Will you take them too?" as everyone look expectantly towards Harry.

HARRY (confidently): "Well – I'm an Indian-ized Bond

so sorry – only work, no womanizing!" and they all shake their heads, not believing a word of what he said.

While the spruced up team at ST was busy churning away creating software, they were surprised by a visit from a Quality Assurance (QA) representative.

SUNNY (bellowing): "Hey Harry, the QA rep is here for code inspection."

HARRY (sarcastically): "Do you'll have a search warrant?" as his colleagues laugh out.

The rep (amused): "Of course we do. We never come unprepared!" And they all chuckle away.

LYNDA (to Harry): "WHY are you so secretive? Do you have something to hide beneath the hood of your code?"

HARRY: "No *re* (dear). I'm just playing my part of 007 – being secretive" while everyone heaves a sigh of relief.

TUSHAR: "Well, good to see you're playing the part but don't take it so seriously."

HARRY (smiling): "So now what is it that you want me to be if not secretive – seductive?" The ladies glare at him.

Once his short deputation for the project was over, Harry returned to SS and the project neared implementation.

Increased testing spewed out more and more bugs. Soon, it began to resemble a Pandora's Box. The entire development team was upset about this…

LYNDA (sarcastically): "Looks like we'll have to conduct a pest control exercise" as our friends all grinned away nervously.

HARRY (infuriated): "That means more and more code reviewing" and Lynda leers at him.

SUNNY: "Of course. If it's defective, then it's got to be fixed."

LYNDA: "As the saying goes – 'testing succeeds when bugs are discovered'."

HARRY (furiously): "That's the whole point. Why can't people write error-free code?" while now everyone around looks weirdly towards him.

TUSHAR: "Life's not perfect Harry. The road to perfection is through difficulties and hardships."

HARRY: "From today, you will be known as Bugs Bunny – the famous Hollywood cartoon character – after your *buggy* work and bunny teeth."

SUNNY: "It's made by Looney tunes which is also what Tushar is – a *loony.*"

TUSHAR (retaliating): "So you think you are a public transport or a parking ticket issuer – issuing me a *bug-ticket* for every bug discovered?" Soon there's more laughter all over.

LYNDA (seriously): "That's not the end in itself. Once you guys are over with the bug-fixing, there are other things to cover too" as they all look strangely at her.

HARRY (curiously): "What's more to cover once the

software is completed – it's *pooja* (prayers)?" and all our friends cackle away.

SUNNY: "She's right. Before the prayers, there's documentation to complete."

HARRY: "Those are design documents that the client won't need – leave alone fathom," and he along with Tushar begin to chuckle away.

LYNDA: "Do you really think they'll be able to use the software without a user manual?"

TUSHAR (glumly): "Oh God. Now either of us will become ghost-writers" as everyone else was flabbergasted at that remark.

LYNDA: "Is it because the code is *haunted* i.e. still has hidden bugs as ghosts?" and everyone guffawed away.

TUSHAR: "Good attempt but we're referring here to the fact that no one else from the team will be around when we initiate that exercise. So, either of us, that is assigned the blessed job, will be working all alone and our environment will resemble a ghost town. To add to that, is the rest of the employees going about their business, like zombies straight out of a horror flick!" Our friends laughed out so loudly that their stomachs started aching.

HARRY (announcing): "Good job Tushar. I'm really proud of the way you've depicted our plight. It's really very difficult to chip away with no one else for company. We feel as though we're externed." Our friends all nod in agreement.

SUNNY (justifying): "I can understand how you feel Harry. We've all gone through that but you must understand the reasons – budgetary constraints" while the both of them nod exchanging knowing looks.

HARRY (countering): "Yeah-yeah-yeah. I can see that. Sending multiple people on-site for the implementation is a cost control exercise?" Tushar nods vehemently in approval to that.

LYNDA: "Don't you realize that these are multiple activities that need to be completed – like installation, end-user training and acceptance. Besides, they won't all be there for the entire duration" as Sunny nods in agreement – much to the discomfort by both the allies.

HARRY: "And what about the member stationed there? Will he join the client company as *dahej* (dowry) after the marriage (contract)?" And they all laugh at that remark.

SUNNY: "That person is a support executive stationed there for a short duration."

TUSHAR: "Why not allow either of us to perform both those roles – document cum support executive?" as Harry too is all excited about that suggestion.

LYNDA: "Both are dedicated full-time roles. We can't merge the two, as both functions will suffer. Good attempt – though!" as they both exchange figh-fives much to the disappointment of the other two.

HARRY: "Even the specs have become so hazy."

SUNNY (cynically): "So why don't you wipe them clean

before looking? For a change, it'll make you see things for what they are!"

HARRY (annoyed): "You know very well I'm not talking about my spectacles – it's the software specifications I'm worried about. They are ever-changing – creating so many problems for us to understand and implement." Tushar nods in approval.

TUSHAR (adding): "And they undergo such radical changes at times, it's like traveling from the east to the west – complete opposites. That causes a lot of increase in time and work – not to mention increase in coding complexity. In fact, such drastic changes should be refused" and Harry emphatically nods to that.

LYNDA: "You see – we need to reason with clients. These changes with business developments and we can't refuse them without risking jeopardizing the contract itself."

SUNNY: "And, if we can't cover their functionality, we're not fit to cater to any requirement in the first place." Lynda is mighty impressed at that attitude of his.

TUSHAR: "Well – let's just hope our next project is a bit easier to cope with."

HARRY (pessimistically): "That depends on whether we get a new development project or a maintenance one." Tushar is suddenly alarmed at the very prospect of that.

SUNNY: "Guys – maintenance projects have their positives too – quick work completion due to mere tweaking of existent code, clarity in specs, existent documentation updation and then even the emoluments are better." Lynda looks on captivatedly towards him.

HARRY: "And what about those realms of code to understand, refurbishing invalidated routines, no clear and complete explanation of the functionality as well as code structures? Sheesh" Tushar suddenly feels sickened at the very thought of it all.

SUNNY (resignedly): "Harry, you are SUCH a bummer that you might even succeed in making a newly married groom (pointing towards Tushar) – headed to join his newly-wedded (and *duly-bedded*) wife waiting for him in their honeymoon suite – utterly depressed" while Tushar begins to join Lynda at first and then Sunny to laugh away at that analogy and even Harry eventually joins in.

LYNDA (confirming): "I love the way you put it Sunny. Seriously guys, although I can relate to everything not being all hunky dory, yet every cloud has a silver lining. You've got to believe that every problem has a solution. Your outlook has always got to be positive and at all times." And they all agree to that ideology.

The leaders were successfully able to nip the unrest in the bud itself before it could have transformed into a mutiny – now they all proceed to wrap up their project work completing their respective assignments in good spirit.

5

UP AND AWAY

Soon, our friends were gearing up to fly overseas on work assignments. While their work permit applications had been sent, they met at a coffee shop to – well – talk shop and to take stock of their vistas for their visas...

SUNNY (enacting): "To B(1) or not to B(1), that is the question" as our friends laugh out at his predicament.

LYNDA (admiringly): "All this tension has surely made a poet out of you!" Everyone easily agrees.

TUSHAR: "I don't understand why you don't want to go abroad, Sunny."

MAITRI: "Coz Sanaa can't join him there" and they all start to tease him.

TUSHAR: "It's not even 6 degrees of separation with the

advancement of today's travel facilities."

SANAA (reasoning with Sunny): "Actually, it's only 3 months of separation and it'll be good for your career, just like conferences will be for mine" as she impresses everyone by her attitude.

HARRY (gloating): "You'll are all *bikharis* (beggars). Your visas are only for 3 months while I've got H-1B – for TWO YEARS" and they're all alarmed at his swaggering.

TUSHAR: "I don't understand why you're going for such a long duration while we're going for such a short period."

HARRY (clarifying): "You see, you have a big team of specialists, so each will be there for short durations playing their part while in my case, I'm all alone and will need to perform multiple roles. That's why the longer duration." of course they all seemed convinced.

MANPRIT (impressed): "Wow. That's big. And how lucky you people are! We'll never get to go out for work, here" He and Maitri wore a disappointed look.

MAITRI (trying to conceal her sadness): "Btw, where are both the groups headed to?"

TUSHAR: "While we're headed for NY (New York), Harry's headed to NJ (New Jersey)."

MANPRIT (coming to terms with the disappointment): "Good ya. You can meet up."

LYNDA (skeptically): "I'm not so sure we'll be able to, as we'll be hard pressed for time."

TUSHAR: "When our leaders briefed us on the work, they insisted that we'll need to work hard. So, I'm really wondering whether we're actually working for the pharmaceutical company *Wockhardt*" while they all burst out laughing.

MAITRI: "Well put. We actually work very hard. If we worked any harder than this, we'd become *hardened* criminals!"

SUNNY: "In such a pressurized situation no chicken gets cooked in the *pressure cooker.*"

SANAA (licking her lips): "The only thing that gets cooked is our own goose"

People were holding their tummies laughing away at the obvious reference to the grub.

Soon their visas arrived and they headed for their respective destinations out of the country. Their initial few weeks went in acclimatizing themselves with the place and surroundings and settling in with their onsite teams. They finally managed to meet up after 2 months at a joint, *jointly*. However, they neither went to NY nor NJ as planned earlier but went to NH instead - New Hope in Pennsylvania...

SUNNY (raising a toast): "A *penny* for your thoughts, Mr. Pennsylvania" as his mates smiled at that.

TUSHAR (amazed): "Gosh! Everything looks so new

around here." They all nod in agreement.

SUNNY: "So what did you expect? Earlier it was NEW York, then NEW Jersey and now NEW Hope. Everything is new, nothing of the old order." They laugh away at that depiction.

He started crooning a Hindi song 'Meter Down' from the Bollywood movie Taxi No. 9211…:

"…

.".. *Yaha pe jindagee kee har khushee* (Here all of life's happiness)

Rupaiya hai ya dollar haiya pound (Are Rupees or Dollars or Pounds).

Hey meter down, down-down-down-down-down…"

TUSHAR (glaringly): "True that we're earning in bucks in Bucks County but we're not hired cabs." That sets them all sniggering.

(And he trails off to chant the title track of another Hindi song from some other Bollywood movie *Meeruthiya*…)

"…

"… *Dollar hoya pound* (Whether Dollar or Pound),

Ho rupya ya dinare (Be it Rupee or Dinar),

Ek din apne pocket mein (1 day they will be our pocket)

Honge ye saare (all of them) …"

HARRY (impressed): "*Waah yaron* (Wow friends). But I'm

supposed to be James Bond na (right)?" and they both nod in approval.

SUNNY (surprised): "Yup. But this is the first Bond I've come across who's averse to women!" They all burst out laughing at that comment.

HARRY: "HOW can you say that? I've never done anything to that effect."

SUNNY: "Exactly. I haven't seen you associate with them either. (Softly) Are you gay?" as suddenly everyone around started looking suspiciously at him.

HARRY (yelling): "*Kuch bhi* (What rubbish)!" and all those who were staring away went back to their respective discussions.

SUNNY: "Then tell us who your girlfriend is?"

HARRY: "I'm not dating anyone at the moment. I'm single."

TUSHAR (butting in): "And ready to mingle."

SUNNY: "I should say ready to import."

HARRY: "But I won't be able to import any beauty, as there will be heavy *import duty*!"

TUSHAR (admiringly): "*Wah* (Wow), what poetry!" as they clap away.

Meanwhile, our friends here met up a few days after Harry returned to his site – in the absence of those departed (overseas!)

MANPRIT (pensively): "How I wish I too had taken that certification that these guys took!" and they all looked at him.

LYNDA (reassuringly): "It's not just that. It's also their aptitude, attitude and ability to take on responsibilities" Manprit is surprised to learn this.

AVIS (adding): "If they can see proficiency in your work, they won't be looking out for any further qualifications. It speaks for itself" while they all nod in approval.

LYNDA: "Never underestimate yourself. Each individual is different and has something unique to offer."

SANAA: "Relax dude. Your time will surely come. Wait in the wings."

LYNDA: "We're all here for each other. And it's only for a few months. Before you know it, they'll be back." All of them attempted to make him feel relaxed.

MANPRIT (regretfully): "Additional qualification always makes us more knowledgeable."

SANAA: "What about work experience? Isn't that the most important factor? Learn to convince them that you have done similar work."

AVIS (comfortingly): "I know you're missing the troika and so are we all here. We've gathered here today and will continue to enjoy ourselves till then." Manprit silently welcomes his gesture.

Soon, Tushar and Sunny completed their work and it

was time for them to return. Harry, though, had to stay back to continue with his. They promptly organized a party to handover the gifts that they'd brought for their beloved friends...

LYNDA (warmly): "Welcome guys. Good to have you'll back."

SUNNY (emotionally): "We really MISSED you guys there." They all exchange pleasantries.

TUSHAR (gesticulating): "He's talking about one person in particular!" while everyone now exchanges knowing glances.

AVIS: "Could that be me?" And everybody starts to glare at him.

TUSHAR: "As far as I know, he's straight. Correct me if I'm mistaken."

LYNDA: "Avis, Tushar's referring to Sanaa" and Avis looks very embarrassed as the others smile away at him.

SUNNY (changing the topic): "Did we miss out on anything while we were out?"

DAVIS: "Well, there's been a discovery while you people were out." They look at him in surprise as does everyone else.

TUSHAR: "And that is?" And they all await Davis' response.

DAVIS (merrily): "Ahem, Avis has a girlfriend in the company Software Consultants (SC)" Everybody breaks into smiles looking at the blushing Avis.

SUNNY: "That's good for you. What's her name?"

SANAA (pitching in): "Avishka."

TUSHAR: "Looks like you really wished (A-wish-ka) for her" And they all laugh away to that.

SUNNY (shaking his head): "No wonder you found out 'cause you yourself are an *Avishkar* (discovery)."

TUSHAR: "So, between both your companies (SC and ST), your future child can qualify for the Scheduled Cast / Scheduled Tribe (SC/ST) reservation."

LYNDA: "Hey – what about Harry? Has he been hitched?"

SUNNY (Nodding): "Not just yet. Wait and watch" as the ladies giggle away.

SANAA (smilingly): "Looks like he has enough time to." And they all laugh out loud at the thought.

TUSHAR (nodding): "Yeah. That's what we've told him too."

SUNNY: "So what's with the completion?"

LYNDA: "Nothing much. We're just signing-off the project, as it's implemented and delivered."

TUSHAR: "Thank God there are no handovers involved."

LYNDA: "What's wrong with handing over completed work to some other member? Do you want to work on it like forever?"

TUSHAR (animatedly): "It sounds like a hold-up job – the stick-up kind."

LYNDA: "I beg your pardon?"

TUSHAR: "Doesn't it sound like "hand over everything?"

LYNDA (shaking her head): "Oh c'mon. It can't be that bad."

TUSHAR: "You haven't an inkling baby! Let me put it this way...

When I'm giving handovers, I feel like I'm on a flyover with all the relief but when I'm taking handovers, I feel like I'm getting hangovers with all the stress!" And soon they were all laughing away.

SUNNY: "True that. They feel like a game of musical chairs - what with all this changing guard of project personnel."

LYNDA (adamantly): "Well – personnel rotation can cause change in team composition but it's more like stepping into someone else's shoes. To draw an analogy, I would suggest following the toilet upkeep policy. Just like how we would expect it to be orderly, we too should take adequate pains to keep it orderly. It's like if you'd like to step into a senior's good shoes as in position, you too should make sure yours are kept good for juniors who'd like to step into yours one day." They're captivated by her response.

They all signed off too and our ST mates were eagerly waiting to be assigned their next projects. However, that didn't happen very soon and it was some time before they met their friends again (after a gap of 9 months) …

SUNNY: "Hello guys. It seemed like a long time away from you all."

MAITRI (sighing). "Yes. We all have been into a lot of stuff."

TUSHAR: "How have been things with you guys?"

MANPRIT: "Slowing down. How was your trip? I heard you people had a lot of fun with Harry."

SUNNY: "Yes. We managed to meet only once, though."

MAITRI (shrugging): "That's natural – being onsite. At least you did manage to meet. So, when is he due to return for a break?"

TUSHAR: "In 3 months' time."

MANPRIT: "What's the next assignment for you guys?"

LYNDA (resignedly): "We're all floaters for now – waiting in the wings for the project to be assigned" Maitri and Manprit were shocked to hear this.

SUNNY: "*Bhatakti aatmaen* (Wandering spirits)" And everyone smiled at the analogy.

MAITRI (joining in): "*Achahai. Mil kar sab ko darao* (That's good. Together, frighten everybody)" as everybody laughs away at that suggestion.

TUSHAR (matter-of-factly): "Precisely what we're doing – scaring people out of their wits" while they sniggered away.

SUNNY (reminiscing): "If Harry were here – being a James Bond fan – he would say scaring the daylights out of people, after the Hollywood movie Living Daylights."

MANPRIT: "Be patient. You will get your projects soon."

SUNNY: "But we do have to meet sooner, though. This time it was an exceptionally long wait."

MAITRI: "True. But since the three of you were out, it wouldn't have felt the same. Now when Harry's back, we can meet again in the next 3 months" Everyone agreed on when their next get-together would be.

TUSHAR: "Maitri, if you have to go overseas, which place would it be?"

MAITRI(puzzled): "Pray, why don't you just enlighten us?" and they all smile eagerly at him.

TUSHAR: "*Georgia* – as you used to love the poem 'Georgie Porgie Pudding Pie' during your childhood days."

SUNNY: "By George, you could even sing that English song 'Georgia on my mind' from the soulful pop singer Michael Bolton" Everybody chuckled at the thought, much to her dismay.

MAITRI: "Tushar, which is your favorite Hollywood actor?" and he looks expectantly at her, as the others look on amused.

SUNNY: "He likes Jean Claude Van Damme" while Tushar glares at him for giving that out, much to everyone's surprise.

MAITRI (pouncing on that): "Just as I'd expected. What else would we have expected from someone who is a clumsy clod? Damn you." And they all burst out laughing at that repartee.

Time passed by when they did some time pass. Next Harry was back in town for a small break and he setup a party to catch up with his old and dear mates...

HARRY (welcoming): "Friends. Nice to meet you'll after a long gap!"

TUSHAR (hugging): "Welcome back bro. Missed you" Everybody greets each other excitedly.

HARRY: "REALLY? Then why did you all meet in my absence?"

SUNNY: "Take it easy, Harry. We were getting bored and wanted a break. If it pleases you, we didn't really enjoy that get-together enough though."

HARRY: "But of course. That's what'll happen if you meet without me."

LYNDA: "Trust me. It's long overdue. That's why it was only a one-off meet and we decided to meet next only once you were back."

SANAA (changing the topic): "Leave all that now. Tell me how you've been."

HARRY: "Enjoying my work but missing you guys immensely" of course they were all glad to hear that

MANPRIT: "Enjoying work – of all the things and that too alone? You're a real freak."

TUSHAR (smilingly): "You must've moved to that famous peppy English song from the pop singer Rihanna called (ahem) 'Work-Work'" while they began visualizing that.

SUNNY (smirking): "Knowing him, a more apt English song would be from the pop band 2 Unlimited suitably called 'The Workaholic'" as now they could relate to that.

HARRY (countering): "At least I'm not an alcoholic like you all and everybody laugh at that.

(Continuing) Assigned a new project, guys?"

SUNNY: "I don't know about the project but we're certainly not floaters anymore."

HARRY: "THAT'S better. I didn't know that you all are yet to be assigned, though."

MANPRIT: "Great. See, I told you, have some patience." They all sneer at him.

LYNDA (hissing): "What great? We have been warming the damn benches since eternity!"

TUSHAR (cursing): "B(h)ench** (a profanity)!" as everyone at first glared at his usage of the expletive but subsequently smiled at its suitability.

LYNDA: "MIND your language, Tushar" as they all look furiously at him.

MANPRIT: "You mean you all are on the dreaded bench waiting to be assigned to the project."

TUSHAR: "Well, I sure was one of the backbenchers, but this is taking things too far."

SUNNY: "This isn't a sport, where you need extra people for good *bench strength*."

MANPRIT (proclaiming): "Take it constructively. Utilize the time effectively" as they all mock at his suggestion.

SUNNY: "Like how, a *Babaji* (Saint)?."

MANPRIT (animatedly): "Assist a team in some other project, upgrade your technical skills, create a new internal project, do some reading, go home early and complete pending things, take some time off, etc. The list is endless..." Everyone's seriously amazed at his suggestions.

TUSHAR (praying): "*Wah. Tussi great ho!* (Wow. You're great)" They all nodded.

SUNNY (smilingly): (borrowing from that famous Hindi dialogue from the Bollywood movie 3 idiots...)

"*Toh fir tumhara tohfa kubul karao* (In that case make us accept your gift)" while everybody laughs away.

TUSHAR: "*Tohfa to Harry laya hoga aur fir gayega* (Harry must've brought gifts and then he'll sing...)"

(He started singing the title Hindi song from the Bollywood movie *Tohfa*)

"*Tohfa tohfa tohfa, laaya laaya laaya* (Gift-gift-gift, brought-brought-brought)."

MANPRIT: "Yeah. Harry, what or rather who shall we say, you've brought with you?"

HARRY (exasperated): "Oh no, not again!" And they all continue to tease him till they wind off.

Well – our people aren't the only ones who flew. Our dear time *flies* too – that too without any ticket, passport or visa. Harry flew back to resume his work after the small breather while the ST guys used up the few months, they had on hand the way they felt was right. Time passed by and they next met up after a gap of six months...

MANPRIT (eagerly): "I hear you guys got assigned after all!" Everyone nodded.

SUNNY (looking relaxed): "Yeah. Phew!"

MAITRI (enviously): "So you all must be enjoying the time together?" And they all exchanged amused glances.

LYNDA (shrugging): "Well – not really, as now we work from home (WFH)" as she hums away the tune of the famous English song by the same name from the pop band 5th harmony.

TUSHAR: "Wfh – *Wtf*!" as the guys laugh away.

LYNDA: "Hey, watch it!"

MAITRI: "But what's so upsetting about working from home, Tushar? You have so many conveniences." They all nodded in approval.

SUNNY: "Like?"

MAITRI: "Saving on travel time and cost, better health, better work – home life balance, adequate rest, effective time management…"

SUNNY (exclaiming): "Spoken like a true *babaji's* (guru's) partner."

MANPRIT: "But why so upset with it? Everybody these days is clamoring for it."

TUSHAR (waving his hands): "No face-to-face time-out with friends, no natural atmosphere, less concentration due to disturbances, more time for work."

MAITRI: "That can be made up for in today's technology age of web conferencing."

TUSHAR: "But one can never replace the experience of being there in person. You see, the grass always looks greener on the other side!"

SUNNY: "Flexi-Time would enable us to get the best of both worlds, to some extent" as they all agree with it.

LYNDA (adding): "Yeah. Travel during non-peak hours, complete errands, chores and get some good rest."

MAITRI (opposing): "Well, you still can't completely eliminate the strenuous travel – though" as they all agree.

SANAA (screaming): "ENOUGH guys. We'll have to take it in our stride." and they all made their way out.

Harry, meanwhile, had completed his two years overseas and was due to return. But they discovered that he got an extension. Since their meeting was now long overdue – as the group had planned it to coincide with his return – they decided to have a small get-together in lieu of a grander party till the time he was actually by their sides.

It wasn't until another Nine long months that he was finally back. Impatiently, they all met up again after he settled in to take stock of the *extending*...

SUNNY (yelling): "What maan? You tell us two years and disappear for almost another year? What's going on in your life?" They all ask him eagerly.

HARRY (pacifyingly): "Nothing at all – except for work. You know how it is. Scope keeps creeping up and we're blamed for being creepy" and they all smiled away at that.

TUSHAR: "How did you manage to pull yourself through this added time and did you miss us?"

HARRY: "Don't ask. It's a long story with a lot of unexpected turns. It was indeed a very tough time for me and you bet I definitely missed you all."

MAITRI: "We aren't really in a great deal of hurry and have enough time to listen to your tales."

MANPRIT (keenly): "Yeah. And we're very interested in knowing the details too."

HARRY (grudgingly): "Ok. Here goes. I actually had 3 extensions of 3 months each" Now they're all surprised to hear that.

SANAA (surprised): "Oh dear! And you must've always felt you're done with and due to return?" And he nods away in agreement.

HARRY: "Guys, that's just the beginning. When the 1st extension was expiring, I had to step out to Canada close by and step back in after renewal."

AVIS: "Phew. That must've been tense."

HARRY: "If you think that was tough, wait till you hear of what followed the next" and they all listened with bated breath.

(Continuing): "When the second extension was about to expire, I was planning to step out to Dubai and come back once the situation had settled. But my visa application was rejected and I was left with no option but to rush back to my dear ol' country in time to avoid deportation!" They all let out a collective sigh of relief.

SUNNY (sarcastically): "If I'm not mistaken, there IS a procedure wherein we're required by way of good practice to keep track of work elapsed vis-à-vis it's duration in line with the progress calendar, isn't it?" as Harry looks snidely towards him for that.

LYNDA: "Exactly what I reminded him about on this melee."

TUSHAR: "All this has to be done by you, Lynda. You

can't really expect him to do all that book-keeping there instead of focusing on his work."

HARRY: "There you go – my boy. That is the same as what I pleaded with them when they tried to castigate me for those sordid episodes."

MANPRIT (curiously): "Anyways, what about the 3rd extension?" And they all listened in anxiously.

HARRY (relieved): "Thankfully, they too were very fed up of extending my stay and stopped extending the work. This time they made sure that it completed well within the 3 months and booked my tickets well before the next expiry date sprung up." They all cackled away at that happy turn of events.

MANPRIT (pensively): "Then why simply seek such small extensions in the first place?" They all agreed to that one.

HARRY: "That was a mis-placed strategy to put pressure on them for the sign-off and to cut-short the duration but it apparently backfired."

AVIS: "Why all that hassle? Ultimately, the authorities would've brought you here only and that too at their own cost." They all laughed their guts out to that remark.

LYNDA: "Are you out of your mind? That would've closed his visa book forever!"

HARRY: "Weirdo! That's the best way to ensure that you're rooted to your country forever – a negative way to show your patriotic nature. It's also a surefire way to be placed under country arrest akin to a house arrest for us high-fliers." And, he banged his head on his desk – much to everyone's amusement and Avis's bewilderment.

MANPRIT (inquisitively): "Lynda, you could have sent me on 1 of the extensions, at least! That way, he would've got some respite and me some exposure."

LYNDA: "Don't you think I tried? The problem was they didn't want to let go of him. They wouldn't have entertained anyone else, so had to stick with him – even though he himself wasn't ready to."

HARRY (tauntingly): "Would you have really survived on my work leftovers?" And they're all disappointed at his brashness.

MANPRIT (ruefully): "Beggars can't be choosers. I would take whatever comes my way. At least I would've got my very first stamp on the passport to show for it. As for your work, it is very thorough and I would really have no problems closing or extending it - whatever may have been the case." And they're all impressed at his attitude on display here.

AVIS: "So how would you guys summarize your experiences till now?"

HARRY: "Work is worship" while they all scoff at his comment.

MANPRIT: "Work is *worth shit*" as our friends all cheer to that remark.

SUNNY: "Work is *warship*." Now it's time for applause from his friends.

Having wrapped up their get-together and the chocolates Harry brought for them, they went back to their respective homes. They finally began to enjoy their work and thus were more relaxed in their lives.

6

LIFELINES AND TIMELINES

Now all of them had earned promotions and increments. While Tushar had become a Senior Developer, Sunny was now a Team Lead, Sanaa was in the position of an Account Executive and Lynda a Project Leader. They got together to celebrate…

MANPRIT (gleaming): "Another grade completed." And they all nodded away in acknowledgement.

TUSHAR (gesticulating): "Passed and promoted to the next level is our performance card." Our friends all smile to that.

HARRY: "Always good to add another number to the result card."

LYNDA: "Harry, how was your trip?"

HARRY: "Draining but it was very good." Our friends all nodded their heads in acknowledgement."

SUNNY: "Good to get the support, eh?."

HARRY (negating): "Well – not all the time, really…" he said to everyone's surprise.

SANAA: "Huh?"

HARRY: "We always had to work on our national holidays while on their national holidays, we'd be having an off." while his friends shook their heads in resentment.

MAITRI: "*Wah, tumhara doodh doodh, humara doodh paani* (Oh yeah, your milk is milk but ours is water)?" as everyone laughs away.

SANAA: "What a dialogue!"

Sunny began belting out an emotional mom's Hindi song from the Bollywood movie *Aakhri Rasta:*

"*Tune mera doodh piya hai* (You have drunk my milk),

Tu bilkul mere jaisa hai… (You are just like me)" and they all burst out laughing.

HARRY (upset): "It's unfair but couldn't get them to accept it. I just had to give in."

LYNDA: "Life's not fair. Still, you could've informed them in advance." And our friends nod in approval.

TUSHAR (looking at Lynda): "But you most certainly are (fair)" while now our friends start looking expectantly in her direction.

LYNDA: "Shut the funk up, Tushar."

TUSHAR (continuing):"Our present positions remind me of a very soothing ballad – an English song 'When love and hate collide' from the famous rock band Def Leppard." They all chuckle away to that.

HARRY (returning to the topic): "Believe me, I had, but

they refused to reason saying that you all have just too many holidays!"

TUSHAR: "You did get their holidays, didn't you?"

HARRY (countering): "How would you like it if I asked you to celebrate your birthday on mine?" They burst out laughing at that presentation.

MANPRIT: "Aptly put."

HARRY: "I used to really get psyched out not celebrating days which we have celebrated for years now and get freaked out on their holidays."

LYNDA: "Yes. It's difficult to fix the yearly holidays even in cross-country multi-cultural teams."

HARRY (going on): "They also wouldn't stretch themselves during deadlines. Most of the time, I've had to wind off for the day." They were all really surprised to hear that.

MANPRIT (pacifying): "Not everybody can work as hard as you Harry. Chuck it, man!" And they all totally agreed to that.

HARRY (sarcastically): "That's not quite what we're told when we miss our submissions deadlines."

LYNDA: "True that. We're expected to put in the hard yards but not give in."

SUNNY: "What's the point of talking about things that won't change?"

TUSHAR (rejoicing): "Amen. Let's raise a toast to our success, instead." They all look for their glasses on the flooded table.

SANAA: "*Sandwich or masala* (seasoning)?" and they all laugh out loudly at that.

HARRY (now more relaxed): "Thanks for bringing me back to this world."
SUNNY (loudly): "As Shakespeare said…"
"If food be the music of life, eat on."
LYNDA (amusedly): "That's 'if music be the food of love, play on'" while they went about devouring their stuff.

Once they started receiving their big fat pay packages, they started splurging on life's pleasures. While someone bought a set of wheels, another one flew a flight of fancy; one of them *covered new ground* by moving into a new place and so on and so forth. After they were done going so gung-ho over their earnings, they got a rude shock when they discovered that their tax liability had increased manifold. Worse was in store when they found out that they would have to invest heavily in tax-saving financial investments in order to prevent taxation from eating into their earnings. Given that they had already booked many goodies, it was indeed very *taxing*. That served as a dampener and they learnt an important lesson that they needed to save a part of their salary not only for tax-saving purposes but also for retirement funds – not to mention for future demands and even contingencies.

One day, Tushar saw Harry entering the HR department at ST…

SUNNY (excitedly): "Tushar, looks like Harry is taking up another project here!" They were all happy to hear that.

TUSHAR (reasoning): "Why doesn't our company employ the bench staff instead of hiring outside guns?" And our friends shake their heads in doubt.

SUNNY: "You've certainly got a point!"

LYNDA: "Because they don't have the relevant skills needed!"

TUSHAR: "So can't they be trained or instructed to get oriented in them?"

LYNDA (disapproving): "That's plausible, I guess. But not practical." Now everyone's surprised.

TUSHAR: "How so?"

SANAA (to Lynda): "Allow me... When a project gets the go-ahead, resources are needed upfront. At times, they are already assigned to another project." Lynda nods her head in agreement.

TUSHAR: "So can't they be trained beforehand?"

SANAA (justifying): "That's like a chicken and egg dilemma - to train for the project or get the project for the trained skills. Often, it's the former."

TUSHAR (proposing): "So why not provide training on different skills to different resources?" This proposition takes our friends by surprise.

SANAA (nullifying): "That increases the training costs – as some of the skills might not get projects" and they all nod their heads in approval.

TUSHAR (satirically): "Oh and I guess it decreases the costs to hire temporary hands!" as they all look suspiciously towards him.

SANAA: "Stop the sarcasm. What's ailing you?"

TUSHAR: "These costs are reducing the profitability

thus affecting our pay-outs." To this, they all agree unanimously.

SANAA (slowly): "Ok... So, what kind of a solution do you propose?"

TUSHAR: "We need to make the team resources upgrade their skills on the job."

SUNNY (cutting in): "That's easier said than done and also not really advisable, as you tend to get staggered time and that will surely affect the quality of training and practice." as they all agree.

SANAA: "Just like staffing, it is a difficult balancing act. Either you're over or under staffed – as the projects signing dates are always uncertain..." They all have a resigned look on their faces as they realize that it's a never-ending vicious cycle of sorts.

LYNDA (gesturing): "Time-out – guys. Let's ask Harry who's just coming over to us." They all look towards him.

In walks Harry and proceeds with them to the cafeteria...

SUNNY (welcoming): "Hey Harry, good to see you. What bring you here – HR travails?" And they exchange pleasantries.

HARRY (announcing): "Hey guys. I have the good news and the bad news as well..." while our friends show mixed reactions to that.

TUSHAR: "Bring it on."

HARRY: "Well, you guys have been chasing me on my love interest and now I actually have one!" They all are taken aback at his frankness.

SUNNY: "Oh really? Who is it – tell us all quickly?"

HARRY: "Well – after a brief courtship period, I'm presently into a relationship with her."

TUSHAR (dazed): "Wow. Talk about catching up with lost time with a vengeance!"

SANAA: "I really hope she's not married."

HARRY: "Nope, she isn't. But I sure as hell am!"

LYNDA (confused): "Whoa. Wait a minute. You mean to tell us that you married and are also having an affair simultaneously in such a short span of time. That's really hard to believe. When did all this happen?"

TUSHAR: "Bird in the hand and also in the bush, eh? Burning the candle at both ends, ha? Ok. So, what's next, Casanova?" as our friends blatantly stare at Harry's cockiness.

HARRY: "Simple. I'll get a divorce shortly." he says to their shock.

SUNNY (disbelievingly): "Huh, I just don't know what to make of this. You're actually going through a marriage, an affair and now a divorce. All this is a real heady concoction – this cocktail of yours. All of this was done while you were away from us. Are you sure about all this?" Everyone wears a really pensive look.

HARRY (convincingly): "I'm decided now but was confused earlier on."

SUNNY (disappointedly): "So how will you clear this mess?" as they all await his response.

HARRY: "My hands are clean. I've already filed for divorce and will be moving in shortly." to everybody's utter surprise.

SUNNY (after a while): "So where does you latest 'flame' stay?"

HARRY (pointing): "Right here!" Our friends look in that direction.

SUNNY: "What?! Does she work here?" and they all try their best to make some sense of all they are suddenly faced with!

HARRY (laughing): "No-no! I mean ST!"

TUSHAR: "How? I still don't get you."

SANAA: "But I most certainly do!" to everyone's total surprise.

HARRY (back-patting her): "Smart gurl!" as they start to look at her.

SANAA (to Harry): "Please enlighten them!" and they're all attention.

HARRY: "Well – the courtship occurred when I was on the project here with you all. This was followed by an affair, which started a few weeks back, after which I was – ahem – propositioned by ST." While some of them who understand it start laughing out loudly, explaining to the others.

SUNNY (deducting): "Oh. Now I get it. So, the divorce is from SS and you're moving in at ST" as they all now nod vigorously.

TUSHAR (eagerly): "So, when are you actually moving in?!" His friends are all smiles now.

HARRY (merrily): "In a week's time!" He said to everyone's pleasure and surprise.

LYNDA: "I suppose there'll be an alimony demand too from SS now" and they all laugh out aloud.

HARRY: "You bet! But I've got my bases covered!"

LYNDA: "How?"

HARRY (smugly): "Like a traditional orthodox Indian. I've promised a marriage. So, I'll be getting a good fat Indian dowry for it. Besides the hike on jumping, I'm also promoted to a Senior Developer and will get a salary revision." Our friends congratulate him amidst all the chuckling.

SUNNY: "Amazing! Well done"

AVIS (dazed): "Wow. What a script. It even has a fairy tale ending. I'm moved to tears to see you'll together!" And everyone guffaws away.

They were all really very happy to discover that Harry will be re-united with them right here at ST. They began talking behind his back while they waited his return…

SUNNY (stating): "Hey guys, I've noticed that Harry's *in-laws* are taking up a lot of his time" and they all seem convinced.

DAVIS (deliberating): "Maybe, those are the dowry demands – a *ghar jamai* (a son-in-law who stays with his in-laws)" while the guys all giggle away.

TUSHAR: "Priceless!" as they all start looking towards Sanaa.

SANAA (firming up): "What utter rubbish!"

LYNDA (supporting her): "I swear!"

AVIS (clarifying): "No. It's true. I've seen him spending a lot of time at the HR," as the ladies breathe easily.

TUSHAR: "Must be procedural formalities – of no-getting a clear clearance!" as they all smiled.

SUNNY (seriously): "Let's ask him, instead of beating about the bush."

No sooner had Harry returned, he was thoroughly grilled by them!

SUNNY (beckoning): "Harry, are they demanding the dowry back?"

HARRY (smilingly): "Oh! Not at all," he surprises them with his answer.

TUSHAR: "Then, what's with the persistent visits?" Everyone's obviously curious.

HARRY: "Nothing much. Just routine induction procedures related stuff." No one seems very convinced with that explanation.

SANAA: "I'm sure there's more to this than meets the eye!"

HARRY: "Never judge a book by its cover."

LYNDA (impressed): "Wow. What a competition of sayings! Don't stop, please continue."

AVIS: "But there's no smoke without fire."

HARRY: "This is nothing but VIP treatment to the *jamai rajah* (son-in-law who is king)."

SUNNY (sternly): "What happened to all that talk about being a big fish in a small sea?" They all hum in approval.

HARRY (deftly): "Well, the sea just underwent a sea of change!" And all our friends laugh out loudly.

SUNNY (clapping): "Wonderful."

HARRY: "So now, I can see myself in a bigger sea."

SANAA: "Wonderful guys. Keep going!"

SUNNY: "But, I still smell something fishy." And he looks towards Sanaa.

Repeating their friends retort, they blurted out together: "Spoken like a true foodie!"

AVIS: "No seriously, something's cooking."

DAVIS: "I think you'll are on the right track."

LYNDA: "What do you mean?"

DAVIS (gesturing to Harry): "Our dear *fisherman* here has just fallen for a mermaid!"

LYNDA (amused): "What. Right here?" as they were all curious.

DAVIS: "Yes, right in these very waters!"

SANAA: "Who's she?"

DAVIS: "Harry, should I spill the beans or would you rather?"

HARRY (giving the go-ahead): "Please do the honors. I've been well and truly hooked – having taken the bait."

SUNNY: "Yeah. And we're awaiting your response with bated breath. C'mon now – out with it! We're a-waiting."

DAVIS: "Well – here goes. She's Harshita from you-know-where!" and there's a buzz all around.

TUSHAR (clenching his fist): "Gotcha. She's from HR!" Everyone's surprised at his speed.

DAVIS: "Bingo."

TUSHAR (warily): "Are you sure this divorce / alimony business wasn't about her?" while now they all became very nervous.

HARRY (surprised): "What're you saying? Not at all!" and our friends feel reassured.

LYNDA (reasoning): "You're right, Harry. That wasn't about her but you can't deny you went through all this settlement business – just for her..." as they all agree with her.

HARRY: "Absolutely, Lynda."

TUSHAR (gesturing towards Lynda): "Love makes you do strange things!" And he made a few romantic overtures and our friends lapped it all up amusedly.

LYNDA: "Back off, Tushar!"

SANAA: "It's 'Love makes the world go round.'"

SUNNY (ironically): "It certainly makes it go *aground*" while they all burst out laughing.

SANAA: "Take a hike, Sunny!" as everyone enjoys this new conflict now.

SUNNY (comically): "Sure thing. Could you be a dear and book a *hiking trip* for me?" and they all burst out laughing.

Their other friends Manprit and Maitri felt that they had gained enough experience and left ITS to join SC. While Maitri joined as a senior developer, Manprit joined as a senior tester. However, they discovered that SC had revamped itself into an IT-enabled services company. There, they met up with Avishka. After exchanging pleasantries, they proceeded to sort out things...

MAITRI (dismayed): "What do we do now, guys?" and both the ladies wore a worried look.

MANPRIT (reassuringly): "Relax. There's enough work even in this space for all of us." But they seemed unimpressed.

AVISHKA (dejectedly): "We're moving AWAY from Information Technology…" Maitri nodded away.

MANPRIT (refusing): "Not really. It's just that we are now into Information Technology Enabled Services. All this will still need software and more." but they were still not convinced by that.

MAITRI: "Correct but essentially we are no different than telemarketers."

MANPRIT: "Say, you could make it really interesting by making different voice modulations to go with your mood, fine tuning your pitch along the way and get back your mojo."

MAITRI: "Hey that's such a lovely idea to make a drab little conversation rather enthralling!"

AVISHKA (feeling a bit better now): "Though, this is less mainstream and current."

MANPRIT (agitatedly): "You mean to say it's downmarket?"

AVISHKA: "Noo. I meant it's NOT upmarket."

MANPRIT: "What makes you say that?"

MAITRI: "Well, for starters it's not as paying."

AVISHKA: "Also, people don't look at it with as much respect."

MANPRIT (amazed): "REALLY? I would think the financials are catching up and they're already at decent levels." Now this piece of information certainly shock them up.

AVISHKA: "That's reassuring."

MAITRI: "There are odd-hours though."

MANPRIT (justifying): "That is the specialty of our industry. Even our so-called rich cousins do work in shifts catering to the time zones of different countries at some point or the other in their careers." Maitri appears to be quite convinced.

AVISHKA (questioning): "So how does one brace for it?"

MAITRI: "You either grace it or embrace it" and they all burst out laughing.

MANPRIT: "Well said, Maitri. To draw an analogy from a Hindi song of the Bollywood movie *Badshah…*"

"Rat ko barah baje din nikalta hai (The day dawns at 12 in the night),

Subah ko chebaje rat hoti hai… (The night starts at 6 in the morning)"

AVISHKA: "Well said!" Maitri however doesn't seem too happy working at odd hours.

MAITRI (doubting): "What about future prospects?"

MANPRIT: "Well, the future's so bright, I gotta wear shades!"

(Continuing) "Seriously, we're learning all aspects of off-shore customer management from inception to service to billability and accountability…" Now they look mighty impressed.

AVISHKA: "That sounds nice too."

MANPRIT: "Besides this career, another interesting option would be the outsourcing business."

MAITRI (uncertainly): "What does that include?"

MANPRIT: "It includes setting up processes that do the outsourced work for smaller organizations in Knowledge Management and other departments like Legal, Human

Resources, Payroll, etc." Now they're dazed.

AVISHKA (excitedly): "So, what you're saying is that these are all systems?"

MANPRIT: "But of course. Why or how else would they work?"

MAITRI (pensively): "So, won't we be moving away completely from the mainstream technology then?" She seems rather confused.

MANPRIT (elaborating): "Enterprise Resource Planning (ERP) technologies are what drive these systems. Though they might not enjoy the popularity of their more famous siblings, they are more paying!"

MAITRI: "Hey, that's very reassuring. We could, after all, still become the sought after specialists."

MANPRIT (educating): "There's also another field where you could specialize – Software Testing" but he realizes that their interests have now been completely weaned by ERP.

Although that field had no takers, still those were reassuring words for them as they went about their work in all earnest, as though they were working for Ernest and Young!

Next, the guys went for a boys' night out. When the gals discovered this, they refused to talk to them. After much persuasion, they grudgingly agreed for a get-together…

MANPRIT (justifying): "Calm down ladies. We just wanted to hang out together to have some good time."

MAITRI (hissing): "So you mean you can't have a good

time with us?"

SUNNY: "Not at all. He means we wanted to have some privacy."

SANAA: "You mean you don't enjoy our company and want to meet without us?"

AVIS (pleadingly): "Gals, we just wanted to have things our way."

AVISHKA (animatedly): "You mean we don't allow you all to do things your way?"

HARRY (defensively): "Guys – no offence, but we wanted to have talks on topics of our interest."

LYNDA: "So now we don't allow you'll to talk about what you want to, is that it?"

SUNNY: "We do things we can't when we're out with you all like boozing and also don't do things that we have to do with you all around like dancing. We tend to discuss sports, politics, religion, etc."

TUSHAR (bravely): "I'm sure you'll have different girlie things to chat about too when you all go out together... like gossiping, shopping, etc. So why don't you all head out alone like us and have your space too?"

Though there is no outwardly response to that veiled jibe, there is a short buzz between the ladies till a response finally comes through...

SANAA (resignedly): "We don't go out together all that much."

AVIS (jutting in): "Then you should. And then why not too?"

AVISHKA: "Actually, we face a lot of abuse along the

way."

MAITRI: "And not to mention the amount of harassment we have to put up with, wherever we go."

SUNNY (lividly): "We can tag along with you'll to fix those bloody creeps."

LYNDA: "Then it won't remain a girls' night out!"

MANPRIT (dejectedly): "Is there no way we can ever tackle this menace?"

MAITRI (disappointedly): "It's becoming increasingly difficult to move around even amongst ourselves."

TUSHAR (calmly): "Can't you all try meeting at someone's home instead?"

AVISHKA: "Even then we have to travel to each other's place."

LYNDA: "Even if we did manage to meet up during the day, returning back from late parties is another scary and risky ordeal."

SANAA (jadedly): "And to think we've been facing this since our adolescent years."

SUNNY: "Have you tried measures to prevent this?"

AVISHKA: "For how long will you be able to ignore the innumerable vulgar invites or stares or even flashing and other repulsive acts?"

MAITRI: "Can you keep hopping around maneuvering anything you carry as a shield against perverts who use every little opportunity to nauseatingly touch us?"

LYNDA: "Will you always successfully be able to dodge out of sight of habitual and permanent stalkers?"

SANAA (remorseful): "We can't concentrate on shopping completely when we have to dodge those repulsive touches while trying out just about everything from clothes to belts to shoes!"

MAITRI: "You forgot about the time when we give alteration measurements as well as when men brush by against us – making it look accidental."

AVIS (anxiously): "I hope the situation does change at work?"

MAITRI: "The lecherous advances never really cease."

AVISHKA (seriously): "And then there's the cell stalking with continuous calling, lewd messages, sexting, etc.

MANPRIT (stunned): "I fail to understand why people resort to such cheap acts."

SANAA (regretfully): "Partially, society is to blame – what with movies glorifying the ignoring of the rejected overtures by the man in pursuit."

AVISHKA: "Here, refusal is NEVER taken as an option and the man's genuine persuasion is interpreted as a forced choice thrust upon us."

MAITRI: "Porn also plays a part in fuelling the basic human need to a full blown desire, like an animal instinct."

LYNDA (dismally): "And to think, people treat these attacks as those initiated by our dressing, jovialness or even consuming spirits. We might be free-spirited in discussing, friendship and even high-spirited letting our hair down to enjoy ourselves but how does that translate into promiscuousness?"

SANAA: "Isn't the same thing when done by a prostitute intentional, whereas – when taken as the same for us regular folk – a convenient interpretation?"

AVIS (matter-of-factly): "These partially or illiterate folks are squarely to be blamed for this sorry state of affairs."

AVISHKA: "I beg to differ. We've even faced fully cultured people indulging in some of these acts."

LYNDA (brutally): "Tell me honestly guys – haven't you ever fancied your chances on spotting a looker?"

TUSHAR: "To be very honest – well – that is just a thought that I'm capable of trying to attract her attention or plain simple I find her or her dressing attractive. It does not indicate intent."

LYNDA (replying): "And if she were to respond positively?"

TUSHAR (blatantly): "I would take it further only if I'm ready and not in a relationship."

LYNDA (attacking): "How very convenient!"

TUSHAR: "If I'm really serious about starting something with her, don't you think I would take more efforts to win her over rather than wait for her cue?"

LYNDA: "Point taken."

TUSHAR (disappointedly): "You underrate me."

LYNDA: "So then you won't gaze at her bust, butt, legs, thighs or whatever else that's supposedly on offer or even her silhouette made out to be a curvy figure? God you men compartmentalize our body so much that activists like Pamela Anderson have to campaign against this body parts obsession."

TUSHAR: "Phew, I'm not blind. How will I assess if she's pretty if I don't even look at her?"

LYNDA (shrugging): "I've no choice but to agree."

TUSHAR: "But what about if she wants to showcase

her voluptuous figure and fall all over me with her provocative dressing and charms."

LYNDA: "Oh. So now – suddenly – you would get ready, I suppose?"

TUSHAR (honestly): "Well – at least I have a right to be tempted, haven't I?"

SUNNY: "Lynda, could you please stop with the test. Tell me instead that basically what you gals are saying is that there's utter lawlessness when it comes to your security?"

SANAA (responding): "Why's the test worrying you so much? Anyways, there's a great deal of lawlessness here – unlike in some other safer countries where it's much easier for women to travel alone."

AVISHKA (explaining): "That's why the reservation in public transportation like buses, trains, metro, etc. is still required by us."

MANPRIT (astounded): "It must be very difficult for people to gain your trust."

LYNDA: "Well – an enterprising few have gained it only to violate it at some of the most unexpected moments – hounding or even demanding favors. So, we can never really bank on it."

SUNNY: "I can only imagine how tough it must be for you all. How difficult it might be to never be able to relax."

AVISHKA (lightening the mood): "You see, that's why we're so alert."

TUSHAR: "It's a sorry state of affairs when we can't protect our own self."

SANAA: "All our problems begin with those damn men

– 'menopause, manhandle, manslaughter, maniac' and the biggest joke of them all – 'mankind' to quote a few!"

AVISHKA: "There seems no end to our problems due to man interfering with everything like 'adamant, demanding' to mention some!"

LYNDA (longingly): "How I really wish that this structural defect could actually be corrected in something like a 'manicure'! Now I realize why we're so perfect, coz he improved on his mistakes with you all!"

MAITRI: "I can think of many ways to dispose them off like 'manifold, manhole, mango' to name a few!"

Manprit(grinningly): "That's because you women cannot survive without men – you all are incomplete without us. You see – *woMAN* also contains man, as does *huMAN!*"

MAITRI (magnanimously): "You see that's why we're super humans. We have to always adapt and sacrifice at various stages of life to work around the limitations that man creates for us until he realizes the folly of his ways."

AVIS (stoically): "Three cheers to women on this women's day. May they lose their travails and lead a happier life – getting the equality they wish for. Hip-hip-hooray!" as the gals raised a toast to that – much to the chagrin of the men who threw menacing looks at him.

SUNNY: "And what about when ladies don't look which way they're going and we're supposed to make all efforts to prevent bumping into them, 'cause they'll blatantly blame us for it?" The gals nod in agreement.

MANPRIT: "What about those women who shove us away, at times using their oversized bags as props, to which we can't do a thing?"

SUNNY (sneeringly): "Also, what about when they willingly and brazenly break queues and even demand preferential treatment?" as now the gals start snickering.

MAITRI: "I guess that's why we're called the fairer sex, along with the tag of the weaker sex..." and the gals guffaw away.

AVIS: "Gosh. It looks like I'll have to eat my own words. You can't have it both ways gals – having the cake and eating it too!" And now the guys roar away.

SANAA: "And we're not just not ready yet to eat humble pie" The gals exchange high-fives, much to the dismay of the guys.

TUSHAR (proudly): "No wonder it's called a man's world" while the guys are now elated.

AVISHKA (adding): "It sure is, but after we the women. See, even your name follows us" and the gals tinkle their glasses to that.

MANPRIT (smugly): "But you all came into this world only after us!" And the guys cheer away.

LYNDA: "That's because man wouldn't have been able to do anything without us."

SUNNY: "So if you gals can get by – all by yourselves don't need us for anything and can do everything without our help, how about reproducing by yourselves?"

AVIS (gulping): "Guys and gals relax. Take it easy. We both need each other. Let's leave it at that and not get worked up over something that's inevitable." Everyone nods in agreement to that.

———❦———

7

EXCERPTS FROM THE EXPERTS

Soon it was time for them to meet up again and they all went out of town for a small overnight picnic. After having their grub at a restaurant, they all settled in for a long night of fun in the lawns where other patrons too were partying the night away in their small groups. This time – though – they had also taken along with them the twins Avis and Davis, as well as Avishka, as their group stood out from the crowd – being not only the biggest but also the noisiest…

DAVIS (noticing the couples): "Hey guys, you should go to those couple joints – now that you'll are all hitched!" and they all agreed.

MANPRIT (looking towards them): "Yeah – like Sunny and Sanaa" as they all looked in their direction.

MAITRI: "Ya and the latest pair of Harry and Harshita."

SUNNY: "Et tu Manprit and Maitri?"

SANAA: "Also you guys Avis and Avishka" as now it was their turn at be looked at.

DAVIS (sarcastically): "Avishka can't complete that pair as she's not really a guy! Make that Avis and Davis" while everybody jeers at them.

AVISHKA: "Shut the funk up, Davis!"

Avis (to Davis): "Stay away from me – you possessive creep!"

SUNNY: "So who's left behind now – Tushar and Lynda? Yay!" as they all clapped.

LYNDA (glaring at him): "Just pipe down, Sunny" as Tushar blew him air kisses.

TUSHAR (starts to sing an adaptation from an old Hindi song of the Bollywood movie *Aulad*):

"Jodi hamari, jamega kaise jaani (How can our pairing work),

...

... *Tumko bhi mushkil, mujhe bhi pareshani* ... (Difficult for you, troublesome for me too)"

LYNDA (agreeing): "Wonderful Tushar, I'm proud of you!" And everyone applauds that rendition.

(Continuing) "Don't you see the pairing linage? Not only don't our names match but they aren't even remotely similar..." and her friends all nod in approval.

After downing a few rounds, they started getting philosophical and getting into the *spirit*...

SUNNY (announcing): "Guys listen up. Let's play an intelligent group game called 'Prop-opponents'" and our friends are pretty interested to understand how to play it.

MANPRIT (curiously): "What's that and how does it go?"

SUNNY: "Well – as the name suggests – it includes two teams – the proponents and the opponents that will slug it out in a debate "

TUSHAR: "I'm tempted to say that it sounds debatable…" as they all laugh out aloud.

SUNNY: "It actually is. The rules of the game are pretty simple. Every player has to propose a point in favor of his team while the opponent will get an opportunity to oppose it without discussing with their group. After that, the proponent will get an opportunity to justify his position with the opponent having to finally agree or disagree to the justification without any group discussions." Even the other guests at the party listened in curiously.

AVIS (impressed): "Sounds good. My mind has already started spinning."

SANAA (inquisitively): "What will be the teams?" and they all could no longer wait to begin.

SUNNY: "Patience – my dear – is a virtue."

SANAA: "Ok, my dear *virtuoso.*"

LYNDA: "Spill the beans."

MAITRI (restlessly): "Yeah – out with it."

SUNNY: "Easy does it. Here goes…

Proponents: - Me, Maitri, Tushar, Avishka

Opponents: - Sanaa, Manprit, Lynda, Avis."

LYNDA: "Good selection captain. No mates, no genders

– perfectly mixed and matched. No favors given, none taken."

AVISHKA (approving): "Can't wait to begin" as everyone gears up.

Soon they all began to deliberate and are ready to begin...

SUNNY: "I love it that today our industry has powered virtual shopping – granting time, space and monetary convenience."

SANAA: "We might have replicated the eye, ear and tongue sensations of the physical shopping, but we are still to replace the nose and touch sensations."

SUNNY: "That surely could happen in the near future with virtual reality."

SANAA: "Agree" as the P's were ecstatic.

MAITRI: "We've improved security and surveillance in today's terrorism age with various high-end gadgets."

MANPRIT: "But it's at the cost of our freedom. We've created a monster in tracking of people and animals besides being even absurdly locked out by our own creations."

MAITRI: "Yes but there are workarounds to such incidental and unintended problems like emergency access. It needs to be well regulated and secured from unauthorized access."

MANPRIT: "True."

And this time the others rejoiced.

TUSHAR: "You cannot deny that we've made life *e-asier* with e-booking, e-ticketing, e-bill payment, digitization, e-admissions and e-governance."

LYNDA: "But it brings with it a new set of mazes where we tend to get stuck somewhere in between. Besides, it takes away the analogue feel with these automated things."

TUSHAR: "It's not like there are no solutions to those glitches. As for the analogues, the world is evolving at a very rapid speed. We need to keep pace with it by moving with the times and release deadwood."

LYNDA: "Ya" and they patted each other.

AVISHKA: "We can now reach out to people and be contacted them from any geography with improved communication like clearer voice and visuals."

AVIS: "It's at the cost of privacy. No personal or private time left – especially when you don't want to disclose it."

AVISHKA: "We can figuratively and quite literally really disconnect, if and when we choose to get away from it all."

AVIS: "I agree" while they shook each other's hands.

MAITRI: "Social networking has enabled us to connect with and keep in touch with both buddies and colleagues regularly, whom we cannot meet frequently."

MANPRIT: "It brings with it the addiction of staying online and connected all the time."

MAITRI: "Moderating it will enable us to use it sparingly

without getting hooked but there's no denying its power and utility."

MANPRIT: "Of course" as now they began mocking their opponents.

SUNNY: "We can now conduct all kinds of teaching, training and meeting virtually, thus saving time and money that would be spent by the tutor as well as that of the audience travelling to the site."

SANAA: "But it brings with it, inadequacies like impersonal experience, time lags, etc."

SUNNY: "There are solutions to those issues like email interactivity, recordings to cover up for those issues."

SANAA: "Yes."

AVISHKA (gesticulating): "Time out guys. Here I would like to say that it also takes out the real pleasures of actual meetings like the food, the networking, interactivity."

SUNNY (strongly): "Agree!"

SANAA: "I just love *mee(a)tings*" as they all burst out laughing.

AVIS (agitated): "Hey admin – we're getting all mixed up here. We can't make out who's on which side. Can you stop this and get back to business, please?" and the O's were very happy to have something going their way finally.

TUSHAR: "Remotely-managed technology enables us to control unmanned devices like in space, surveillance, potentially dangerous situations, for comfort during travel."

LYNDA: "But it can also spiral out of control and cause greater collateral damage like the unauthorized drones."

TUSHAR: "There are always teething troubles in every invention which can be eventually sorted out – like authorizing state use in sensitive areas like defense and disallowing private usage like for pizzas, etc."

LYNDA: "I agree."

And the P's were happy to be back in business.

MAITRI: "A lot of embedded software runs in entertainment gadgets like TVs, household equipment like ACs and business machines like scanners – enabling us to use them suitably."

MANPRIT: "It also complicates things – what with having to decide which of the plethora of buttons we have to click."

MAITRI: "In today's age, each one of us moves in the direction they have chosen. Life is now all about the choices you take, no longer that were thrust upon you."

MANPRIT: "That's right" as they were at it – celebrating again.

AVISHKA: "3D printing is enabling us to save on manufacturing costs, giving flexibility, personalization and dynamism in many sectors like medicine, construction, F&B, architecture, engineering, machinery, furniture, etc."

AVIS: "This hurts the industry when these gadgets replace human labor like cooks, carpenters, engineers and such others."

AVISHKA: "Though it would impact some of the human services like carpentry and foods, it could still enable customization in them for e.g. by creating personalized furniture, dishes personalized with chosen toppings, etc. It most certainly can create an impact in the rest of the automated services besides replicating human body internals for advancing medical science."

AVIS: "True that" The dominant team now began prancing around.

TUSHAR: "Another precedent is increased, improved, effective and affordable storage in electronic media like phones, computers and even portable devices like chargers, memory cards, etc."

LYNDA: "But this miniaturization is at the cost of durability and sturdiness."

TUSHAR: "Yes. But there are solutions like taking greater care of these things than earlier in return for compactness."

LYNDA: "Yes" And our losing team started getting sadder by the minute.

AVISHKA: "All organization level functions like Purchasing, Delivery, Billing, Accounting, Operational Expenses, etc. can be linked up together through technology to give all stakeholders a realistic and complete picture."

AVIS: "Down time here would be killing."

AVISHKA: "Not having a system to project the real time status at all times would be an even greater killer in today's quick world."

AVIS: "True."

MAITRI (jutting in): "Here, we would also like to add that all Call Management, Incidence Management, Mass marketing, etc. can also be managed effectively through technology."

MANPRIT (also barging in): "But this will force us to be hooked onto technology all the time."

MAITRI: "This is the fastest and most effective way to tackle enterprise-level geographies, volumes and dimensions."

MANPRIT: "Yes!" Now the losing team started getting irritable with their opponents' antics.

AVISHKA: "Technology also enables us to protect and safeguard these huge volumes of data that we generate at other remote locations with backup and failover techniques."

AVIS: "Technology fuels innovation. See the route from oil-based lamps to electrical ones and from bulbs to CFL to LED to provide energy efficiency for all gadgets to save on energy consumed and reduce the carbon footprint."

AVISHKA: "Yes but it's at the cost of frequently having to shell out more for high-end gadgets."

AVIS: "Well – it's the price we have to pay for evolution!"

LYNDA (getting worked up): "Hey-hey, how can you both just blatantly switch sides like this? This is nothing less than cheating" as they all were up in arms over the move.

SUNNY (laughing): "Easy does it, guys. It's only a game. Let's not take it so seriously. It's such that in our passion we forget which side we're on."

Suddenly, they realized that all the eyes and ears were only on them – people staring on with total amusement, as they had gone overboard in their talks. So, they decided to go down a bit…

TUSHAR: "Technology has enabled us to speed up input not only with mechanisms like scanners and electronic import of data but also to capture data faster with text-to-speech, Swype, etc."

LYNDA: "But this has resulted in our handwriting becoming poorer – rather if at all we do write something in the first place."

TUSHAR: "There are other ways and means to keep writing a bit – like to-do chits for various things like errands, chores etc. in addition to signing cheques."

Lynda: "Ok" she said amidst wild celebrations.

AVISHKA: "The credit rating that we get due to the high salaries our industry pays helps us to avail loans and credit cards easily and at a much lesser age than our predecessors."

AVIS: "With that comes job uncertainty where we could be fired even before we have finished uttering the word, unlike our predecessors."

AVISHKA: "Life is not certain anymore. We just have to make the most of it 'cause however hard we try, nothing and nobody in this world is indispensable except the maker."

AVIS: "Totally agree" as they started raising toasts.

MANPRIT: "GPS Technology has enabled people to locate and reach complicated destinations with great ease and comfort – even providing updated alternate routes as well as durations."

MAITRI: "It also has made people behave like rudderless ships – diminishing any possibility of acquiring any semblance of a sense of direction when not possessing a network signal" and our friends tend to go with her contention.

MANPRIT: "Just think about how it has helped people overcome their limitations of having no basic sense of directions and travel confidently without having to depend on strangers who could turn out to be unreliable." Now she has no takers for her view.

MAITRI: "Well - if you put it that way, none of us would possibly disagree."

SUNNY: "People. I love the power that technology yields today so much so that I'd love to sing that pioneering English song – 'I've got the power' from the pop band Snap."

SANAA: "Guys. Don't forget that we have not empowered; only enabled these services because of internet which is the real backbone."

SUNNY: "How very true. Delivering most of these facilities, illustrating their usage etc. has only been possible due to the power of the internet and the usability of gizmos."

SANAA: "Yes. Finally, we have something going our way" as now it's the turn of their opposition to celebrate.

MANPRIT (butting in): "Technology has been no saint though with the invention of paver blocks. It has only caused a lot of injuries due to uncertain leveling and overall darkness due to power-saving lamps, especially to the elders" Some of his friends readily agreed.

SUNNY (restraining him): "Hey – you're out of line" and they all started murmuring.

MAITRI (volunteering): "I'll take that, Sunny. While it may be true that there is generally more darkness on the streets than in earlier times, proper laying could've made things better with both the pavers as well as them lamps" as they all cheered her response.

LYNDA: "Do you guys have more ammo or are you done?" followed by rhetoric chants from the opponents "Give up, give up, give up..."

MAITRI (after checking with the others): "We're done" amidst crazy celebrations from their opposition.

AVIS: "So who's the winner?" and the opponents started absurd thanksgiving routines.

SUNNY: "Well – each one of us is a winner in his or her own right –"

MANPRIT (interrupting): "No. the real winner is the Sanaa. She snatched it for us in the very last round" while they all start applauding her.

SANAA (humbly): "First of all, I would like to thank God, my parents, my teachers, my seniors. I would like to dedicate this award to the real winner – the Internet. It would suffice to say that this child of technology has now become its father." Everyone burst out laughing at her mock thank you speech.

TUSHAR (whispering): "How I wish I could shut up her pompousness!" while Avis relates to his sentiment
AVIS (emphatically): "Just like every major invention comes with a price, the mobile – which is the enabler of technology, harnessing the power of the internet – comes with the tag of being responsible for the loss of innocence in children." All of them tend to go with that.
SANAA (approvingly): "I couldn't agree more. With more and more people handing out their mobiles to children to quieten them, they have begun throwing even more tantrums – not to mention misusing them." Initially she's very serious but subsequently grimaces on seeing the both of them exchange smiles after the knowing glances

People were truly amazed to see the output and were finding it hard to believe that this wasn't a business seminar and that the people here were not rival business parties!

Soon, another round of promotions came up. Tushar and Harry traded positions with Sunny and Sunny with Lynda. While Tushar, Harry and Maitri became Team

Leads, Sunny was now a Project Leader and Sanaa a Key Account Executive. What about our poor old Lynda? Well, call that a rich Lynda as she became a Senior Project Leader – our generation of leaders! It was business as usual after one of the leadership camps...

TUSHAR (elatedly): "Wow. It feels great to finally become a leader."

HARRY: "I was already a team lead in my earlier jaunt!"

SUNNY (shrewdly): "That was superficial. This is the real thing."

HARRY: "What do you mean, Sunny?"

LYNDA: "Sunny's right, Harry. That was with less responsibilities; this is with much more."

HARRY (clarifying): "No Lynda. At that time, I was doing more work than I'm doing now."

LYNDA: "We say this because the scale's bigger here."

SUNNY: "Accordingly, the tasks are commensurate to the team size."

HARRY: "Oh ok!"

TUSHAR (surprised): "But things look so different now."

HARRY: "How is that so?"

TUSHAR: "Suddenly, we realize we should let go of trivial issues that we developers have, like being possessive of the code that we write, reluctance to re-use someone else's code, unwillingness to go through someone else's written code, non-readiness to code in the prescribed manner..." and they all look on in appreciation.

HARRY (poetically): "*Waqt ka takaza hai, umar ka nahi* (Sign of the times, not age)!" and they all laugh out loud."

SUNNY (proclaiming): "It comes when more responsibility is given. We rise above our own shallow reservations to maximise the collective team's output." And they all nod.

SANAA (agreeing): "That works for us sales professionals too, when we try to work jointly on cases, rather than trying to claim or grab possession of a prospect" while they clap gently.

SUNNY (thankfully): "It's good that ST sends us to such leadership seminars. We gain a lot of knowledge on leadership skills, not to mention the awesome spread" and they all agree.

SANAA: "Yeah. And also make new friends along with trying out new cuisines" as they all laugh out loud at the 'Foodies'.

LYNDA: "It's essential to network with other professionals to understand their situations, experiences and learn from them."

HARRY: "Yes. Nowadays, there's a lot of synergy between different organizations that can be used to collaborate on hybrid needs."

TUSHAR (excitedly): "It sure feels nice being pursued by recruiters!" Naturally, he is not the only one who loves it.

LYNDA: "Enjoy it for some fleeting moments – while you can. You'll soon get fed up!" Our friends all look at her strangely for the comment.

TUSHAR: "It's nice for us guys to be chased – for a change. You gals have had so many guys in hot *pursuit* for years!" while the guys burst out laughing.

SANAA: "What are you grinning at, Sunny?" as Sunny stiffens and they enjoy seeing her silencing him.

HARRY (seriously): "It's difficult to get a team to complete their work on time." And they all shake their heads vigorously.

SUNNY (contending): "That's where planning and execution skills matter. Our work teaches us how to deal with markets dynamics." Now they're all impressed.

TUSHAR: "Dealing with clients is another pain altogether." With that, they all tap their glasses.

LYNDA (philosophically): "You have to develop the trait of interacting with customers."

HARRY: "Interpreting documented requirements are hard to visualize."

SUNNY: "You have to be pro-active to acquire the domain knowledge to propose the complete solution." Suddenly our people now start to pay more attention.

TUSHAR (reminiscing): "Work was so simple when we were juniors!"

LYNDA: "We need to be more responsible as we grow. It's just like a tree. As it grows, each part needs to perform more functions to support its size and stature."

TUSHAR: "But why should we not specialize?" A few of them agree with him on this.

HARRY: "If leaders don't know multiple disciplines, how will they lead? Do you want to just become a Subject Matter Expert (SME)?"

TUSHAR: "Point to be noted milord!" as they all laugh at his words.

SUNNY (changing the topic): "How was your sales

seminar, Sanaa?" They all looked towards her for some inputs.

SANAA: "It was good. It spoke about sales and business maximizing techniques." They all shook their heads – some in approval some in regret.

TUSHAR (confessing): "Leadership techniques don't come easy to me. I'm a soft-spoken and very hands-on person..." They all look at him – not sympathetically but *simply pathetically.*

SANAA (explaining): "Even if you aren't a natural leader, you can work on your persuasion skills." They all applaud her suggestion.

LYNDA (elucidating): "You'll head a team that owns requirements, execution and implementation. You'll get advice, though, from other resources like analysts, architects, etc."

With that, everybody had begun to make a move and they returned back to their work.

After a few days, to everyone's surprise at SC, Tushar jumped ship and joined a consulting firm Total Consultants (TC)...

HARRY (updating): "Did you'll hear about Tushar moving? Wasn't it a bit too fast?" They all nod their heads.

SUNNY: "Yeah. And that too was done at a very fast and furious pace!"

LYNDA (shrugging her shoulders): "Should've hung

on. Maybe something special would have headed his way here, had he been more patient" and they were all surprised.

AVIS: "Here, he would've definitely learnt more – given that he's relatively raw in leadership."

AVIS (closing): "Let's meet him and find out."

Soon, they arranged for an urgent get-together to ascertain it…

SUNNY (excitedly): "Hey Tushar, you disappeared without even telling, leave alone meeting us. What happened?" and they were all ears.

TUSHAR (replying): "Things happened so fast I thought I will let you'll know later, as you all would understand." But they all refused to see reason.

HARRY: "We were worried about you – whether you're fired or what?"

AVISHKA: "Why did you leave here and join there?"

TUSHAR (trying to change the mood): "Let's have some fun. Why don't you all hazard a guess?"

AVIS: "I know why. *Bacche ko daraa diya* (The kid has been frightened off)" And they all burst out laughing.

SANAA: "Are you insinuating here that 'I' drove him away?!."

SUNNY: "Take it easy – Sanaa. He's just pulling your leg. Maybe he wanted to experience the thrill of pursuing those pursuits."

MANPRIT: "Maybe he wants to go away from you, Lynda."

LYNDA (emphatically): "I'd never have stopped him in any case..." but of course none of them believed her.

TUSHAR: "At least if you would have proposed to me, I would've hung on!"

LYNDA: "In your wildest dreams! It's more likely you gave in to the charms of your *pursuer.*"

TUSHAR: "No. I'm faithful to you, Lynda" as they all hoot for them.

LYNDA: "Stop that right now and tell us the real reason!" as they all eagerly awaited the reason.

TUSHAR (happily): "Well, they made me an offer I just couldn't refuse" as they were all surprised at that.

SUNNY (excitedly): "You had better prospects HERE. You missed the project incentives!" They were all astonished.

TUSHAR (dejectedly): "Unfortunately, our law allows us to marry only 1 person at a time and you know who that is" and they all burst out laughing.

HARRY: "Well, he had spent 4 years here. So it's ok, I guess."

LYNDA: "All the best to you there Tushar from all of us here."

TUSHAR (overwhelmed): "Thanks a lot guys. Your wishes mean a lot to me."

And the friends all went their respective ways.

After a few months, they received a jolt when they heard that Tushar had switched jobs again. Once again, they decided to check on him to know more...

HARRY (unable to hide the surprise): "My dear friend

Tushar, again?" And they all look on eagerly.

TUSHAR (apologetically): "Sorry guys you'll heard about this from elsewhere and not me. I've just joined Software Consultancy and Software Testing (SCST)" while a hush fell over.

HARRY: "Chimp, you think you're a *jumping* jack?"

TUSHAR: "I think Tarzan is a better tag."

SUNNY: "No. You're a *B(h)ungee* (Scavenger) Jumper!."

TUSHAR (clarifying): "I'm not THAT smelly, really."

AVIS: "But why-why-why?"

TUSHAR (elaborating): "Well, I found their offer irresistible."

SUNNY (grooving): "I'm sure he must've sung that English song "Simply *Irresistible*" from the pop singer Robert Palmer" And they all laughed out aloud.

MAITRI (butting in): "And guess what guys? Harshita has joined him there" and they all stopped in their tracks.

HARRY: "Stop and settle in. There will always be offers. You need stability now."

TUSHAR: "But the grass is always greener on the other side."

SUNNY: "It will look so, to a *grasshopper*!" while they all burst out into peals of laughter at that.

LYNDA (agreeing): "Well elucidated, Sunny."

And once again they all decided to get going and went about their separate ways.

8

BOYS TO MEN

After a few years, their carrier graphs started moving further. Harry and Maitri exchanged designations with Sunny to become a Project Leaders while Sunny changed designations with Lynda and became a Senior Project Leader. Lynda was now a Project Manager and Sanaa an Account Manager. They decided to meet up and celebrate...

HARRY (elatedly): "Finally, I've crossed the level from a programmer to leader."
SUNNY (merrily): "Congrats and welcome to the leaders club. Why, even Lynda and Sanaa have now reached new levels. They're now Managers!"
HARRY: "Wow. That's great."
LYNDA: "What's new at your end, Tushar?" They all looked at him as they awaited his reply.

TUSHAR: "Once I've eaten something, I'll have something new at my end..." and they all laugh away to that.

LYNDA: "Oh Really, Don't tell me coz that's really crap!"

TUSHAR (responding): "Amazing. To answer your earlier question, you're speaking to a Technical Architect!" They were all really happy for him.

SUNNY: "Amazing. Congrats bro. You've worked your ass off for it."

SANAA: "More good news, Manprit?"

MANPRIT (excitedly): "You'll need to digest some more sweets! I'm now your new Testing Manager. I have just about accepted an offer from your company to join them." They were all happy to hear this news.

SANAA (congratulating): "Lovely to have you with us. But when did you shift to testing?" Needless to say, our friends were all ears.

MANPRIT (replying): "I was never far away. I have always been drawn to testing and then picked out automated testing." Everyone was intrigued by his choice.

SANAA: "Refreshing! Congrats."

MAITRI: "There's more of the good news to go around. I'm joining in too as a Testing Leader."

SANAA: "Splendid. Let's all raise a toast to all of us. Here's to all our promotions (raising the toast)! Even bread toasts or some roasts will do..." she said amidst all round laughter.

LYNDA: "May we all continue to progress and earn many more new promotions!" as they all whistle away to that.

HARSHITA: "Today we've got good news all in a heap. Ok – here goes – heap-heap hooray!"

HARRY: "Good one, Hershey."

TUSHAR (teasingly): "Oh-oh! Hershey... so very intimate!" Having got a chance, our friends now hoot away at them.

HARSHITA: "Please shut up, Tushar!"

MANPRIT (softly): "Harry, have you reached first base yet?" And everybody stiffens at that remark.

HARSHITA: "WHAT'S that?"

MANPRIT: "Er, I just informed him that the base of the first table is shaky." while our friends were in splits.

HARSHITA: "Oh c'mon. We all know what you're getting at. You shouldn't be so pesky."

MANPRIT (defending himself): "Well – I've seen that you all have not just eyes, but even hands as well other body parts for each other!" And everybody is really shocked to hear of their brazenness.

HARSHITA (maintaining her position): "So? What's it to anyone else?" They all could only stare at her forthrightness.

TUSHAR (cooling things down): "Nice to see these celebrities unfazed by media coverage during their PDA (Public Display of Affection)" That got everyone smiling at the analogy.

LYNDA: "Coming back to what we were discussing – now that we're having such varied skills – we could start our own company."

SANAA: "Actually, yes!" while gradually, a few others nod their heads in approval.

SUNNY: "Now we can say that we've all moved from 'boys to men'."

LYNDA (countering): "Why not 'girls to women'. Why do you'll always have to be sexist?" and all the ladies cheer loudly.

SUNNY: "Aree baba (Oh God), it's just a saying. It denotes the same as per the gender."

HARRY: "Exactly. Don't worry we're not going from boys to women or even from girls to men" while all the men laugh aloud.

SANAA (sarcastically): "Very funny."

MAITRI (changing the topic): "All the best to all in their new responsibilities." And everyone raises their thumbs to that.

HARSHITA: "Anything that you'll miss from your old responsibilities?"

SUNNY: "Spoken like a true HR-ian."

HARRY (answering): "I'll miss working alongside the team" And our friends got sentimental.

SUNNY (for once – agreeing): "True that. I faced the same dilemma" and everyone was surprised by that remark.

TUSHAR (eagerly): "What was your experience like?"

SUNNY: "I even faced ragging at the hands of my team on a couple of occasions!"

HARRY: "Oh really? How's that possible?" as all our friends look forward for more juicy details.

SUNNY: "Once when I was entering the team work area, I distinctly heard someone saying 'The Lizard's here'. When I confronted him, he said he was speaking of the popularity of the gaming tool Blizzard!" while they all roar away in laughter.

HARRY (justifying): "What goes around comes around!"

TUSHAR: "That's got to be love." His comment intrigues them all.

LYNDA: "Would you please care to explain how?"

TUSHAR: "'Cause they say that love makes the world go round" and everyone bursts out laughing much to her dismay.

MAITRI: "Go on Sunny and tell us also about the second instance."

SUNNY: "On another occasion, they started hissing away and when I asked them, they said they're impressed with the popularity of the Python language!"

HARSHITA (firing another salvo at Sunny): "The shoes on the other foot now."

SANAA (reminiscing): "This is called instant Karma. Remember your good ol' days?" All our friends vigorously pat her back at the thought.

LYNDA: "Our experience is probably the worst. We're practically out of the team!"

SANAA (seconding): "Hmm. We can only track it now..." as everybody nods their head.

MANPRIT (agreeing): "True that. The Project Leader is the one who really leads the charge." And they all agree.

LYNDA (sadly) "We won't be in touch with active development anymore." Our friends suddenly realize how tough that can be.

SUNNY: "You'll now have to focus more on the management part."

TUSHAR (excitedly): "And you're also rid of documenting that blessed time-shit" And everyone laughs away to that comment.

LYNDA: "Don't just look at it as a mere management thing. It has the power to assist you in case of conflicts as well." Our friends suddenly realize its significance for their own selves.

TUSHAR: "Just like maintaining the captain's log in the Hollywood science fiction classic television series 'Star Trek...'" our friends look at him with squinted eyes "... just like the famous exotic character of Mr. Spock."

SUNNY: "You could also call it the Cockpit Voice Recorder (CVR) in airlines that records everything." And they all begin to imitate airlines personnel now.

LYNDA (defending the timesheet): "Sunny please. It can even serve as a historical log to justify the time spent on activities, especially when things don't complete as scheduled."

TUSHAR: "Is it? You got me there. That's really handy. I could actually use it!" and our friends are stunned to see such a quick conversion of a non-believer.

SUNNY: "Tushar – *tu hai bada Hushar* (Tushar – You are very clever)."

SUNNY (to Lynda): "You can only wear formal suits now!" as the guys seem happy with that development.

LYNDA (countering): "That's only for you guys! For us gals, we can still be a bit casual about it," and the gals cheer on.

TUSHAR (smilingly): "As you'll are in relationships, is it?" while now again it's the guys that laugh away.

LYNDA: "Just back off, Tushar!"

TUSHAR: "Why? Are you bursting crackers from your mouth only?" All of them burst out laughing.

MANPRIT: "While you guys can at least get to work together in teams, Tushar and I will only be able to function like independent consultants."

MAITRI: "Why so?"

TUSHAR: "You see – we're specialists. So we're the experts with the most expertise."

SUNNY: "You're also the least earning resources..." to which they all applaud.

LYNDA: "Well put, Sunny!"

MANPRIT (clarifying): "Total earning wise – yes but not on per hour basis."

HARRY (perplexedly): "How so?"

TUSHAR: "That's because our services are only required for some time. Hence, we turn out expensive if deployed all the while."

MAITRI (observing): "How Lucky! You'll aren't stuck to one team and get to work with everyone. I'm really jealous of you."

MANPRIT: "That may be true but then we also don't get any sort of continuity."

HARRY (deciphering): "So you'll are like fire-fighters. Come, solve a problem and go!" Our friends just couldn't stop laughing at the analogy.

TUSHAR (countering): "Not exactly. We're more like preventive insurance to ensure that everything is covered. Not having us over could make things hit you badly." And they all applaud his response.

MANPRIT (agreeing): "I think your development stage was more of that kind. People would invariably create a fire in their work and as a summoned fire-fighter, you would invariably be putting it out for them." The others all continue laughing.

HARRY: "WHAT! You think our work is akin to putting out a fire?"

SUNNY: "It's supposed to be a compliment. Your work is a rage!"

HARRY: "Is that supposed to be in a good sense or like a road rage?!" And our friends smile away.

LYNDA (clarifying): "Positively, it indicates that you were so quick and precise in your work that not only you never got stuck, you could also diagnose the problem in others work and even get them out of their mess."

SUNNY: "Now you're making him out to be some kind of a surgeon."

HARSHITA: "Not necessarily. Your precise moves would've made a sports player, an accountant or even an artist proud!"

HARRY (adapting a famous Hindi movie dialog): "*Tareef pe tareef. Wah wah* (Compliment begets compliment. Wow)!"

SUNNY (deflating): "*Chup be*! Woh Tareekh per tareekh tha (Shut up. That's date begets date) as they all laugh out.

Aur bola to Tariff pe Tariff, matbal bill bhi ayega (If you speak more, then it will be tariff on tariff meaning even a bill will be sent)" They all chuckle away.

MANPRIT (appreciating): "*Nehle pe dehla* (One-upmanship)!" and our friends applaud the contest.

TUSHAR: "*Nahi. Aaj pehle pe dusra* (No. Today one round after another)!" as they all raise their glasses to that.

HARRY (raising a toast): "Cheers to me!" amidst a lot of clinking of glasses.

SANAA: *"Tum saale bevde log ghum fir karke drinks par h: aaoge* (You bloody drunkards sooner or later invariably come around tc drinking)" which the ladies readily agreed to.

TUSHAR: *"Aur tum log khane pe* (And you people to food)."

HARRY: "Please allow me a decent defense…

At least I'm a fire-fighter. Sunny is that punk from the heavy metal music band Prodigy that sung the famous English song 'Fire-Starter'" and they all laugh out loudly.

SUNNY: "NOW what have I done?"

HARRY: "Guys, hasn't he done enough work to justify that tag?" To which everyone answers an emphatic YYEESS in unison.

SUNNY: "Actually, trouble-shooter is an even better description for you, Harry."

HARRY: "If I'm a trouble-shooter, then you're a trouble-maker" Of course our friends agree to that tag too.

MANPRIT (fanning the flames): "That would make you'll sworn enemies."

HARRY: "I don't know about enemies, but he certainly does swear a lot and it's not for God."

SUNNY (countering): *"Saale, tu bhi koi dudh se dhula nahi hai*! (Bloody, you aren't any saint either)" while they all were excited to see their efforts at fuelling the fire become successful.

The tussle continued for some time and eventually died

down like it always did. Ultimately, they wound up and went back to their respective places.

After a while, Lynda and Sanaa were inducted by their company into some management training program…

LYNDA (satisfied): "Good learning, this."

SANAA (contented): "Yes. We can put it to good use."

LYNDA: "Neat techniques to ensure that one can keep close track of the project."

SANAA: "But there are so many headaches to take care of."

LYNDA: "True. Quoting, Planning, Work Allocating, Financing, Invoicing. Phew!"

SANAA: "And for me Forecasting, Budgeting, Work Allocating, Pipelining, Accounting."

LYNDA (grimacing): "Estimating the project size, Assigning staff and Receivables Collection are the biggest troubles."

SANAA (frowning): "For me, Estimating the Order Size, Frequent Company Information Sending and following up on Progress Stage. It's an SOS for me too!"

LYNDA: "Come again? Sorry, I didn't get you – SAVE OUR SOULS?" Sanaa laughs out loud.

SANAA: "No re (dear). Same Old Situation both in terms of headaches and troubles."

LYNDA: "Oh. It's good that we have a dashboard to give us a birds-eye view."

SANAA: "Yeah. The snapshot gives a complete synopsis."

LYNDA (enlightened): "I'm pleasantly surprised to

see the amount of work done by a Project Manager – especially after hearing how free a Project Manager is – from those PM jokes." They both smile at the realization.

SANAA (agreeing): "True. I also used to feel that while we sales professionals are actually doing all the field work, the bosses are so free."

LYNDA: "And that's not all. We have to collect metrics too in order to get closer in our guestimates! It does look like we'll still be called 'metric-passed!'" And they both laugh out aloud again.

SANAA: "Sometimes, I do feel as though I'm some kind of event organizer – arranging for so many things at the same time."

LYNDA: "You took the words right out of my mouth."

SANAA: "And there are certification courses to make you all look like doctors who hang them out to impress patients."

LYNDA: "Well, you see we are actually curing their pain!" and Sanaa guffaws away at the comment.

SANAA: "But our job is more important than yours. If we don't get any orders what will you'll do?" she asked seriously while Lynda's pretty surprised at her remark.

LYNDA: "Well, that's like the chicken and egg story. If we don't deliver, what good is your order?"

SANAA: "Are you saying that your job is more important than mine!?" And Lynda is now worried at her approach

LYNDA: "I didn't quite mean it that way."

SANAA: "So what exactly is your point?"

LYNDA: "I'm merely mentioning the point that both are equally important. How will your sales complete if we don't do our job?"

HARSHITA (butting in): "Sorry guys, but I couldn't help overhearing your conversation!" They both turn and look in her direction.

SANAA (covering up): "It's ok. We weren't really caught in any serious work – just the thought of it!" as Lynda mocks away at Sanaa.

HARSHITA (asking): "Oh ok. So, continuing in the same vein, should we get the resources first or the orders?" Lynda is startled at her participation.

LYNDA: "The same holds true for staffing as well. To answer your question, well, it's really a mix of both."

SANAA: "True, that. We need to have a skeletal team which has to be augmented after orders start trickling in."

HARSHITA: "Aptly put!"

SANAA (curiously): "So what've you been up to, Harshita?"

HARSHITA: "Finding the right candidates, ascertaining that they're hired within the stipulated timeframes, ensuring that they stay put and even verifying why they're jumping" and the both of them are quite impressed by her reply.

LYNDA: "What's ails you?"

HARSHITA (pensively): "At times, we can't find the right prospect. When we do find them, they're not receptive. Also, the ones that want to join in don't qualify. Once they're finally on board, we've to keep some from jumping again. Let's just call it a mission impossible."

LYNDA: "That's like running a children's nursery where

you have to always keep an eye on what the mischievous children are up to" while they all burst out laughing to that wonderful analogy.

SANAA (sighing): "That's tough. What about administration, salaries, motivations?"

HARSHITA (elaborating): "They have their own pressures – especially during increments and keeping up the attitude is tough in times when business is down" as they all nod away in acceptance.

FARIDA (a finance department person joining in): "Guys, you're missing another important facet here – finance!" and they all turn towards her.

SANAA: "How do you mean?"

FARIDA: "With all your respective business generation, delivery completion and commensurate revenue; without financial planning – no organization can function efficiently."

HARSHITA: "What's your routine like?"

FARIDA: "Well – getting both budgeted and incidental finance requirements from departments, rationing them from generated revenue or saved funds, investing part of surplus revenues and computing profitability for financial health…" while they all seem satisfied with her update.

LYNDA: "Now YOU tell me Sanaa – is HR or even Finance any more or less important than Sales or Delivery?" as they all murmur away.

SANAA: "I hate to say this but I'll have to admit defeat here. I now understand how every department is important. Of what use is all the business generation and completion if we don't have the right people hired or, are able to manage its generation effectively?"

HARSHITA: "EXACTLY. The long and the short of it is, we all need to work together" while they nod their heads in approval.

FARIDA (signifying her approval): "A women!" which was followed by infectious all round laughter.

And the ladies continued to laugh out and cheered for a wonderful bonding moment! After the program completion they went about their respective routines.

9

FITTING THE PIECES TOGETHER

Now that they were all settled in at work, it was time for them to again follow a fashion in their lives. It was the fashion of getting married!

The first to walk down the aisle were Sunny and Sanaa. Not to be outdone by them, Manprit and Maitri followed suit in a few months. Harry and Harshita decided to get all knotty and following in hot pursuit were Avis and Avishka. Everybody had a lot of fun at each of those wedding ceremonies during that year.

This kinda broke up the group, as the couples started spending some – well - house-hold time. So Tushar and Lynda decided to organize a picnic. Looking at them spending private time *publicly* they remarked…

TUSHAR: "Guys, this is a public get-together, not a private family outing..." to everyone's sudden rapt attention.

LYNDA (echoing his sentiments): "Exactly. We're missing all the fun that we all used to have together."

TUSHAR: "You people have started bringing your home to work."

SUNNY: "So what? You'll also take your work home with you, *na* (right)?"

LYNDA: "What about our team here? Why are you guys ignoring that?"

MANPRIT (justifying): "We aren't (doing that). It's just life's demands" as both the singles nod grimly.

TUSHAR (proclaiming): "Do all that at home!" and Lynda backs him on that.

HARRY (arguing): "But we're busy romancing at home, so the only time for all this is here!" which was followed by hoots from the singles.

LYNDA: "Here – only *bromancing* is allowed, nothing else!" while the singles laugh away.

AVIS: "It's we who've missed out on the fun times, lately" as the singles are delighted to make at least one of the couples come around.

TUSHAR (to Avis): "Not to worry. We'll make up for lost time."

SUNNY (announcing): "All right listen up. I have an interesting rhyming game which I call 'Hashit' we can all play now!" Soon our friends are all ears.

MANPRIT: "Huh. What's that game all about?"

SUNNY (explaining): "Everybody will draw out a chit of

technical tool names, read it out aloud and come up with whatever comes to their minds instantly."

MANPRIT: "Sounds interesting."

Harry starts staring at Harshita…

HARSHITA (surprised): "What?" and now all our friends start to look at the both of them.

HARRY (suspiciously): "I suppose the name has nothing remotely similarly to my Harshita here?" as they all look towards her laughing away.

MANPRIT (casually): "Tushar – why don't you too follow us in getting married?"

TUSHAR (smilingly): "I don't want to drown so early in life by taking the *plunge*. After all, marriage can be a real *cliff-hanger*" and everyone's in splits at that comment.

LYNDA (adding): "It's also not good to reach the wedding altar for your *alter* ego" as they all just can't seem to stop laughing.

SUNNY (with a wave of his hand): "A mere coincidence Ok now – folks – let's start!" while they all gear up.

TUSHAR: "So how do we play it?"

SUNNY (responding): "Patience. It's very simple. Let me explain. Let's sit around in a circle. Everybody will rapidly shuffle the chits in the bowl, pick out one chit, read out, tell what it reminds them of and pass on the bowl. Understood?" as they all shook their heads vigorously.

It was Harry who was first in line. He took the bowl from Sunny and shook it well…

HARRY (starting off): "I got Perl. Umm – it never grew outa its *shell*" as everyone smiles away.

TUSHAR: "Visual Basic – for the *hearing impaired*" and our friends laugh away to that.

SUNNY: "Cold Fusion – from the cold war days."

LYNDA: "Ruby – Works only on Tuesdays because of Ruby Tuesday!"

HARSHITA: "Mainframe – only the frame is left now as it's no longer a *mainstay!*"

AVISHKA: "Y2K – Y 2 make such software?!"

AVIS: "Developer 2K – it never really developed!"

MANPRIT: "DOS – (singing away selected lines of a famous Hindi song from an old Bollywood film) ...

DOS(t) dost na raha! (A friend never remained a friend)" They all guffaw away.

SANAA (laughing away): "Thick client – your client is very *thick... in the head!*" Our friends grin.

MAITRI (smilingly): "Hadoop – *Usne data ka saara market hadap liya* (They've grabbed the entire data market share)!" while they all nod away acceptingly.

SUNNY: "Interesting *na* (right)? (Checking the bowl) Well – we're almost done with the first round. We've got 5 more chits to draw."

LYNDA: "It's a riot. Say – why don't you guys go for the remaining chits? We'll egg you on!" and they were all rearing to go.

SANAA (mouth-wateringly): "Slurp!"

HARSHITA (shaking her head): "Watch what you say, Lynda. There goes the foodie! Control my dear friend - control."

SUNNY: "Clipper – it *clipped* its wings!"

TUSHAR: "Dbase – I always watch THE base!" and the ladies look angrily towards him.

MANPRIT: "Borland – it's such an awful *bore!*"

HARRY: "Scrum – you *scumbag!*"

AVIS: "EJB (Enterprise Java Beans) – *beans, oh phooey* – just as we used to hear Donald Duck go in our childhood!"

SUNNY (emptying the bowl): "Hey – last one to go, would any of you gals want to take that?" Lynda volunteers to do just that.

LYNDA: "Alibaba – *aur chalees chor* (and forty thieves)."

SUNNY (fervently adding 2 more chits): "Guys, I just remembered 2 more words. Are we all game for this?" and our friends all gave a definite aye to it, as they continued having a lot of fun.

HARSHITA (philosophically): "ESOP (Employee Stock Options Plan) – I wouldn't only liken it to what obviously comes first to most of our folk's minds. Rather I would link it to the Aesop's fables that we've grown up learning, simply because the former have made their own folklore history in our industry just like the latter" as they all smile – not at her intellect – but nervously at their reminded stock positions.

AVISHKA (smilingly): "Delphi (gesturing out to Sunny and Sanaa) – this truly is food for thought – lovely desserts in *Kulphi* (an ice-cream) or even *Barphi* (a sweet)" and this tickles everyone's funny bone as well as sweet tooth.

SUNNY: "Wait guys. There's one more here. I'll go for this one" while everybody's all ears.

SANAA and **MAITRI** (protesting): "Hey – wait a minute. It's our turn now" as they all are with them on that.

SUNNY: "Believe me. This is apt for us guys. So, here goes..." and our friends try to prevent him from proceeding.

(Continuing) "SAAS – (as he composes himself and sings to the tune of the popular Hindi song '*Taal Se*' from the Bollywood movie *Taal*)"

"... *Saas pe aas lagao* (Pin your financial hopes on your mother-in-law [for dowry])."

TUSHAR (continuing to the same tune):

"... *Par uske paas mat jao* (But don't go too close to her)."

AVIS: "But what if she's a sassy *saas* (mother-in-law)?"

AVISHKA (replying): "*To tumhari sans band kardenge* (Then we'll stop your breath)" and everybody guffaws at that.

Our dear friends had a wonderful time there and returned. After a couple of years, they got promoted even more. Lynda moved up the manager chain to become a Senior Manager while Sunny and Harry became Project Managers, Tushar a Solution Consultant and Maitri a Senior Project Leader. Both Lynda and Sunny started talking shop...

SUNNY (questioning her): "What are you currently into?"

LYNDA (replying): "We'll – I'm in charge of setting up a practice" she says with a very satisfied look.

SUNNY: "Even after being so senior, why do you need to *practice?*"

LYNDA: "Good one, Sunny. It's a specialized centre –

Centre of Excellence (CoE)."

SUNNY: "That's good. After so much of practice, we're bound to be experts in that space."

LYNDA: "Yeah! Very much so" as they exchange high-fives.

SUNNY: "Btw – what's the resource utilization like?"

LYNDA: (Mouthing the popular Hindi dialog from the classic Bollywood film *Deewar*): *"Aaj mere pass sab kuch hai* (Today I have everything) – Architect, Analyst, Graphic Artist, Developer. *Tere pass kya hai?* (What do you have)"

SUNNY: "Mere pass MAIN Developer hai! (I have the MAIN developer)"

LYNDA: *"Woh to sharable hai, na* (That's sharable, right)?" Now she's really worried.

SUNNY (smugly): *"Nahi. woh sirf mere saath rahega!* (No. That will remain with me only)" as he watches her grimacing.

LYNDA: "I hope you're able to factor in all activities in your plans?"

SUNNY: "Obviously. Would you like to look at this one?" And she goes through his plan.

LYNDA (surprised): "What's this – you're going to kick your client?" She begins to smile at that.

SUNNY (responding): "WHAT. How could I? That's the kick-start of my campaign!" wondering what she's getting at.

LYNDA (correcting): "That should be kick-off and it's not your campaign – it's your project" She just can't stop laughing at his error.

SUNNY: "Ya-ya – whatever!"

LYNDA: "This requirement is floated through a tender,

right?"

SUNNY (making faces): "Yeah. I hate them, though" she notices him frowning.

LYNDA: "Why do you detest it so much?"

SUNNY: "They take a very long while to crack and progress is generally very slow. At times, not only deposits but even payments are held up. It's a real strain on every granule of our resources." He scratches his head in memory to those times.

LYNDA: "They're not all that bad. Sometimes, though, we do face those pressures."

SUNNY (befuddled): "Is that so? Then I think surely you must love that classic English song 'Love Me Tender' from the famous yesteryear pop singer Elvis Presley" while he still continues to writhe away at the very thought of working on tenders.

LYNDA: "Incidentally, this is cloud-based and I know that you just love the platform..." Lynda smiles and quite suddenly, he's a transformed man.

SUNNY (swaggering): "Yeah, very much. I feel like a God – high above the *clouds* – with humans below typing away on their gadgets while we up here show them the same stuff in different form-factors. Just like how every religion has a God at its center" while he's completely lost in those *clouds*, much to her amusement.

LYNDA (impressed): "Wow. What an analogy" and she chuckles – having made him come around.

SUNNY (querying): "And which revenue model do you prefer?" He's suddenly all charged up now.

LYNDA: "The rental 1 wherein we charge monthly and

recover more than we could've charged in a fixed price deal. The client feels like he's getting a loan on EMI!" as she rubs her hands gleefully.

SUNNY (amazed): "Great. Even I believe in that model but I'm really surprised on hearing from you that we could make more money out of it" and they both seem contended.

They had had enough and now it was time to close their shop. Soon, they met up with their other colleagues at a discotheque…

HARRY (pleased): "Good to see everyone moving up the value chain!" he says after exchanging pleasantries.

SUNNY (merrily): "And our tiffin's have started getting tastier post marriage!" as our friends agree to that.

MAITRI: "How very true. I'm loving the spread laid out at lunch!"

SANAA: "I for one love the desserts that Android names their versions even more – cupcakes, donuts, éclairs, ginger bread, ice cream sandwich, jelly beans, kit kat, lollipop. Wow. I keep reminiscing about them and have each of these one by one. I can't even think of the I-phone."

AVIS: "Why? Even that one is apple which can be had as an *apple pie*." All the Apple fans support him.

SANAA (proudly): "But that's not the apple of my eye *na* (right)?" as everybody applaud that repartee.

SUNNY (poetically): *"Isliye tumne Nokia ko bhi No Kiya!* (That's why you even said no to Nokia)." Our friends cackle away.

HARRY (matter-of-factly): "Actually – we're having more junk food now. Our moms used to make us healthier tiffin's." They all nod their heads away in acceptance.

SUNNY: "Yeah but those weren't tasty like the present generation ones."

HARRY: "That's why we're heading towards obesity!" Once again our friends agreed.

Avishka just walked in, spotted them and joined in…

AVISHKA (loudly): "HI, guys!" as they all wave out to her.

MAITRI (pleased): "Hey Avishka, good to see you."

AVISHKA: "Well, you'll be seeing more of me. You see, I've also just joined ST!" Our friends look at Avis for his reaction and he's really surprised at the sudden attention.

LYNDA: "Wonderful. A love and her lover are ultimately united!"

AVIS (calming everybody): "Hey-hey – easy does it" as they all try to pit them together.

Suddenly they got swayed by the English song playing 'Wiggle' from the pop singer Jason Derulo, left their seats and went to the dance floor – *wriggling* to its tunes. Soon, they wound off and went their ways. After a few months of work, while they were aimlessly idling away…

TUSHAR (exasperatedly): "All this analytics at work reminds me of our school days when we had questions called 'Give Reasons' to explain our reasoning of everything" as they all let out a loud laugh at that analogy.

MAITRI (eagerly): "And we had to do 'Match the Following' to match resources with tasks, problems with solutions, etc."

HARRY: "'Who Said to Whom' we have to indicate when we're validating requirements."

SUNNY: "We also have to 'Fill in The Blanks' when collating those requirements."

LYNDA (contemptuously): "All this effort really comes to a big naught when the boss starts to play 'State Whether the following are True Or False'" And they all snicker away to that scathing remark.

MANPRIT: "Seriously. We got all that education but no practical knowledge. We can't utilize that in our everyday work lives…" while they all lament the state of their primary education.

HARSHITA: "That might be securing us jobs but not how to work there."

SANAA (anxiously): "We need to have an overhaul in this from mere assessments to actual projects."

AVISHKA: "Yeah. That sure as hell would make it at least interesting and exciting, instead of drab and monotonous."

AVIS (shaking his head): "Presently, it's all about recollection. Anyone who can retain the topic a day before the exams without even understanding it and can reproduce the same in the best possible way, is rewarded for his grasp, as opposed to someone who would've understood it better."

(Continuing): "This makes a mockery of attending lectures and taking in all the explanations. Even after being absent from the class throughout the year, a student can still top the class merely on the strength of what he vomits out on the answer sheet!" They all nod away in approval.

AVISHKA: "To coin a scientific formulae – performance measured is directly proportionate to the volume of pages written, with speed working as a catalyst."

AVIS: "The color green (money) does a litmus test of negating your theory just proposed by enabling submitting the required 'matter' (answer sheet) or even getting the desired result (certificate) without so much as even attempting the experiment!" Our friends all laugh away at that hypothesis.

Our intellects didn't even realize just how they've grown, as they effortlessly moved away from comparing those two stages to be actually commenting on the very system that's not only produced them, but given them the name, fame and successes.

10

THE LULL BEFORE THE STORM

A few years passed, as more promotions came through. Now, Sunny had become a Senior Manager while Lynda was now a Vice President. Soon they met up...

SANAA (observing): "Maitri, you don't seem too well?" and they all look towards her.
MAITRI (confirming): "I'm slightly under the weather" while our friends grimace at her plight.
SUNNY: "So you're blowing *hot* or *cold*?"
SANAA: "We're not talking about the *climate* here."
MANPRIT: "It's too early to start *blowing* the trumpet, though."
SANAA: "Yay. So, it's true – as I'd expected. Congrats!"
SUNNY: "What???" and all the others too couldn't exactly comprehend what was happening.
SANAA: "*Aree* (Oh), dumbos, she's expecting!" as now it

actually dawns on most of them.

SUNNY (baffled): "Ok. So, what does she want?"

SANAA (aggressively): "You fool, she's expecting … a baby!" as now he finally grasped it.

SUNNY (relieved): "Oh. Then say that she's pregnant! This expecting business is confusing. She could be expecting guests, gifts, anything!" while our friends were in splits – much to the grimaced look on his face.

And they all proceeded to congratulate and wish the happy couple…

MAITRI (curiously): "Hey, what about you guys? Any update" while she and the others look eagerly towards Sanaa and Sunny.

SUNNY (smilingly): "We're in total control of the situation" he says to everybody's amazement.

MANPRIT: "Huh. What does that mean?"

SUNNY: "Weirdo's, it means we're planning for one" as now most of them understood.

MANPRIT: "Oh, that's good news for us all" as now they all look towards him in amazement.

SUNNY: "How is that good for *you*?" as Sanaa and Maitri both are intrigued.

MANPRIT (irritated): "Don't you'll see – it's good that they'll have a baby" and they burst out laughing.

SUNNY: "No – you moron. If we're on family planning aka birth control, how can we have a baby?"

MANPRIT: "Can't you have it via many of the other ways like adoption, artificial –."

MAITRI (changing the topic): "Hey, btw, guys have you heard anything from Avishka?" while everybody shook their heads.

SANAA: "No. It's been quite a while. They haven't been in touch. Maybe they're also cooking up something – like you guys Maitri!"

HARSHITA (seriously): "They sure have *cooked* up something and it's definitely more than a storm in a tea cup" to everyone's utter surprise.

MAITRI: "What kind of storm?"

HARSHITA (resignedly): "Well – problems have been brewing there since awhile now" as our friends were still waiting to hear the problem.

SANAA (acceptingly): "True but then who doesn't have problems?" and they all readily agreed on that one.

HARSHITA (sadly): "It's more than just that." Now these words worried them all.

MAITRI: "Now you're scaring us."

HARSHITA: "Well – they've scared the hell outa me!" They all begin to murmur at this comment.

SANAA: "Can you PLEASE tell us what it is?"

HARSHITA (taking a deep breath): "Well – they're separating!" to the utter shock of everybody.

SUNNY: "I've heard of their partying ways but their *parting* ways is just too bad!" and our friends were shocked at his insensitivity.

SANAA: "SUNNY – it's most inappropriate of you to say such things at such a time. That's just too bad, guys!"

SUNNY: "I'm just trying to make it light. What more can we do about that?"

HARRY (suddenly realizing): "Oh. That's why Avis hasn't been responding to my pings. I thought he's tied up."

MANPRIT: "Shit. That's too bad! Maybe we should try and patch them up."

SUNNY: "That's 'make them patch up', not patch them up – as though they're some material. It looks tough, though, from the outside. Both are strong characters and won't agree easily but we could still try."

HARSHITA: "We'll try and help them along. So, what's with the rest of you'll?"

SANAA (loudly): "Hey guys – looks like the stork is going to visit Harshita and Harry!" as they're all eager to hear more.

MANPRIT (puzzled): "Why. Have they kept some special stuff at their place?" to which all our friends burst out laughing.

MAITRI (embarrassed): "No-no Manprit" while he still has that surprised look.

MANPRIT: "So then is it their new pet?"

SANAA: "No, they're getting a pet of a completely different kind."

MANPRIT: "Sorry, I don't follow you."

HARRY: "Neither do I, Manprit!" to which all our friends continue to laugh out – at first softly but gradually louder.

MANPRIT (offended by now): "Can someone please tell me what this stork business is all about and would you'll please put a stop to all that constant giggling?"

MAITRI: "Ahem – they're in the same category as us!" to

which realization instantly dawns on him.

MANPRIT: "OH. Now I get it. Why couldn't you say so earlier? And what's this stork business? After all, they are going to have their own baby – not adopting it, na (right)?"

HARRY (chuckling): "Aptly put, bro!"

They all managed to get Avis and Avishka to patch up their differences and all was well again. After a few months, the world economies went through turbulent times. As business started slackening, they started facing grave difficulties in maximizing client revenue. They decided to have a low-key party...

HARRY (anxiously): "How can we survive without our variable pays?!" And they all agree.

MANPRIT (commenting): "Yeah. To top it, we have hardly anything left in our take-home pay. With everything being taken out, it should be called *taken-out* pay!" as they all smile at his wry humor.

HARRY (worried): "This is no laughing matter. This is serious business!" All his friends nod their heads in agreement.

MAITRI: "It's becoming tougher to live within our means."

SUNNY: "Exactly. After providing apps on EMIs to the world, we have started facing the music – like the American music label *EMI.*"

HARRY: "Most of these are things we can't afford to buy outright – hence we fall into the trap."

MANPRIT: "Don't forget, our families are going to grow soon to add to the expenses."

SANAA (trying to motivate): "In these *hard* times, we need to have more of hard sell."

HARSHITA: "But then, the things that we sell are soft!" and they all chuckle away to that.

TUSHAR: "We need to increase our income streams to compensate for the financial shortfall."

AVIS: "If Farida were here, she would've been proud of you, Tushar! Spoken like a proper finance personnel."

LYNDA: "This too shall pass!" while our friends shrug their shoulders resigned to their fate.

HARRY: "Lynda – in case you've forgotten, we've completed all our *grades* ages back!" as his friends burst out laughing.

LYNDA (prophesying): "Life is a test at all stages."

HARRY: "There goes the philosopher again. When I see that advertisement that shows people caught in the wrong jobs, I seriously think only about you!" And soon they can't stop laughing at that remark – visualizing her in each frame.

MAITRI (making a point): "But seriously, we need to hang in there. These are tough times – indeed" to which they all agree.

AVISHKA (trying to change the mood): "As they say – tough people don't last, tough times do…" while they all find her glitch pretty hilarious.

TUSHAR: "You got that all wrong. That's supposed to be 'tough times don't last, tough people do!'"

SUNNY (changing the topic): "Hey guys, anyone in touch

with Davis?" as they all start looking at each other for a response.

MANPRIT: "No. I guess none of us have seen him around for ages, now."

HARRY: "He hasn't kept in touch nor responded to my pings."

AVIS: "Seems like he doesn't want to be part of our group and we cannot force him. Maybe he doesn't enjoy our company anymore…" They are all confused.

SANAA (thinking out aloud): "But why so?"

AVIS: "He used to always feel that Avishka here has taken his place beside me. Maybe that's made him stay away…" to everyone's surprise.

AVISHKA (upset): "Whoa. That's the weirdest thing I've EVER heard" while our friends try to pacify her.

AVIS: "I'm sorry but I feel that might as well be true. He does miss our closeness since I've started sharing more things with you."

AVISHKA (charged up): "You make it sound as though, not only were you'll in a relationship, but that I was the reason for your break up!" as everybody is too tongue-tied at that remark to even attempt to say anything.

AVIS (defending): "Well – we sure were very close friends before you came along into my life." And our friends were really caught up in this mire.

AVISHKA (aggressively): "What makes you say you'll WERE close friends? Aren't you still?"

AVIS: "I for one surely am but am not quite sure about him."

AVISHKA: "Is he gay?"

AVIS: "Oh c'mon Avi. You know better than to cast aspersions on him."

AVISHKA: "In that case, what then makes him demean your friendship?" as they all now begin to understand her reasoning and anxiously await his response.

AVIS: "Not getting to spend enough time with me."

AVISHKA (calmly now): "But we all have gone out together...and you'll have been out together, too" And they all nod their heads in confirmation.

AVIS: "He feels things have changed quite a bit."

AVISHKA: "That is certainly very true but is he talking about you particularly?" while that's followed by a buzz all over.

AVIS: "Well no, but he misses the days we used to hang out" and now they all began to see the reason behind his absence.

AVISHKA: "He should understand that you're married now and naturally you'll have responsibilities."

AVIS (pained): "He's hurting and can't get over this stage." And they're all disappointed at this development.

AVISHKA (justifying): "He's got to get into his groove. I for sure have and always will welcome him but it seems that he expects only you and doesn't accept me yet!" Now they all rally around her.

MANPRIT (gulping): "I hope he's not the reason for your differences" while they all shake their heads in disbelief at him for sticking his neck out.

AVIS: "No way, man. We just had a few other things to sort out."

SUNNY: "I see that you all have made the effort to comfort him but to no avail."

HARRY: "Yeah. You should let it go lest it spoils your equation again."

AVIS (feeling sad): "It's a pity to see him wallowing…" while they all wear an understanding look.

AVISHKA: "How I wish we all could get him to come around but despite all our efforts, nothing seems to be working."

SANAA: "Hope he'll find a soul mate soon. Looks like a complete loner, now."

HARSHITA: "Yeah. Wish he or she whoever fills that void will bring him back to us again."

MAITRI (disagreeing): "I don't know if it'll pan out that way – given that he's just disappeared. Who knows, he may even find a partner who might be a loner just like him" as our friends shake their heads at his plight.

On that note, they parted ways. No-no – I mean they left for their respective homes, not separated. One of the friends – though – did get away from them. It's tough sometimes, to make people understand the real picture. They're so caught up in their own view that they stop seeing reason. After a few months of struggle at work, they met up again at a small joint…

LYNDA (eagerly): "Sanaa, what's the forecast like?" and they anxiously await her inputs.

SANAA (smilingly): "I'm a sales professional – not a weather bureau person!" as they all laugh out.

LYNDA: "I meant SALES forecast."

SUNNY: "There is a likelihood of a few showers in certain parts of the city!" to everyone's utter delight – while they reminisce on the insipid weather report of the earlier years when TV had just made its appearance.

SANAA: "Nowadays, even the traffic beat on radio sounds like that blessed weather report!" Everybody laughs away at that analogy.

TUSHAR: "You couldn't even have called that weather report a forecast. It was more like a hypothetical statement – more like a probability."

MANPRIT (to Sunny): "And that too coming from a hypocrite like you!"

SUNNY: "What hypocrisy did I practice, you hippopotamus?" and by now everybody's enjoying their slugfest.

MANPRIT: "You're a real *hippy*, Sunny!"

AVISHKA (stepping in): "Attention people, can we please stop calling each other names and focus on the REAL issue here?" And they all quieten down.

LYNDA: "Wow. That's tough talking! So, what'll it be, Sanaa?"

MAITRI (barging in): "The real news is that Avishka and Avis are *expecting*, so congratulations to the both of them!" and all of them proceed to wish the couple heartily conveying their best wishes.

AVISHKA (continuing): "We were derailed. Now to get back on track – what'll it be, Sanaa?" as her friends were in rapt attention now.

SANAA (announcing): "Well – there are indications of a slowdown from market analysts..." There are sighs all around from everybody.

AVIS: "That's just too bad!"

MAITRI: "Enough of living life in the fast lane. We need to slow down."

TUSHAR: "Means?"

MAITRI: "We'll have to curtail our spending to be in-line with the circumstances"

None of them seem happy to hear that.

MANPRIT (countering): "Oh God! That's too difficult to do!" And they all agreed.

LYNDA: "She's right. We can't always be high-fliers. We have to be grounded at times" to wide-spread booing all around her.

SUNNY: "How can we survive without all the good things in life – things which we've worked so hard for?"

SANAA: "Just like how we all used to before we achieved this fair bit of success here…" to which Lynda nods her head in approval.

TUSHAR (grimacing): "You mean to go back to those glum old days. Yuck!"

AVISHKA: "These times won't last forever, you know!?"

LYNDA: "Exactly. Just how do people from the lower strata of society get by?"

SUNNY: "Well – this translates into widespread cuts in our spending's."

MANPRIT (pointing to the ladies): "Including your beauty treatments!" to their utter surprise.

MAITRI (denying): "No way! We can't have that. We can save on other purchases like gadgets…" as now it's the turn of the guys to disapprove.

AVIS (speaking in favor of the guys): "We only need to spend on essentials and that leaves such additional things out!" And now the gals disagree.

AVISHKA: "These are essential for us. We can't survive without them. We'll be grounded. Can't go out looking like that!" while the guys laugh out aloud.

SUNNY: "You'll have completely twisted essentials to suit yourselves!"

SANAA: "Will you'll be up to taking us around without our make-ups?" And that suddenly got the guys thinking.

LYNDA: "Good line of attack."

AVIS: "Well – you can do some basic get-up at home itself."

AVISHKA (disapprovingly): "You won't like that one bit and we'll be relegated to the home. You will be going to your parties all by yourselves!"

MAITRI: "Yeah. You will be only too embarrassed to take us along!"

SANAA: "Not only for parties, even those small errands you will have to do all by yourselves!"

AVIS (gesticulating): "Ok-ok. We get the message! At least try and regulate it" amidst wide cheering from the girls.

MAITRI (celebrating): "Woo hoo! We win!" and the gals start dancing.

SUNNY: "BUT you will have to cut down on the outfits and hairdos."

SANAA (surprised): "Oh no! I guess you spoke too soon, Maitri" as now the ladies starting chatting amongst themselves.

AVISHKA (resignedly): "Well – I guess we'll have to choose some things over the others!" And now the guys seem happy.

MAITRI (agreeing): "We really don't have a choice." And this time, the men are seen rejoicing.

LYNDA: "All of us will have to cut down on individual entertainment and only do group activities!" to which they all agree together for a change.

SUNNY: "That's the harsh truth!"

AVIS: "Not only for all of us here but especially for the harsh people Haresh aka Harry and Harshita!" as they all burst out laughing.

MANPRIT: "Seriously. We'll even have to curtail some of these frequent group parties, including ours obviously too and also ration trips in order to stretch our salaries over the entire month" and our friends find that rationale rationalistic.

SUNNY: "We'll likewise have to hold multiple investments – as now there won't be much of a surplus!"

LYNDA: "Yearly memberships too will have to be done away with!"

MAITRI: "We should also start using shared modes of travel like public transport, car-pooling, etc. which is also good on the environment along with good company instead of travelling all alone."

SANAA: "Even unnecessary electronics purchases (gadgetry) will have to be reduced."

AVIS (forlornly): "Alas, we'll be separated from the best things in life which (unfortunately) *are anything but free!*"

MANPRIT (cheeringly): "But the one thing that we have in abundance is love" to which there's unrestricted widespread approval.

SANAA (sentimentally): "Exactly. Just as the brute of a ballad – an English song from the lovely rock band Scorpions by the name 'Love will keep us alive' symbolizes!" And they all agree to that.

LYNDA (preaching): "True. Such times really tell us how much we love one another!" as they all smile at her statement.

TUSHAR: "Say, how would you possibly know that without experiencing it, Lynda?" while our friends laugh at a hesitant Lynda.

LYNDA: "Take a hike, Tushar!

SUNNY: "Also follow-up on it as swiftly as it's announced, before she decides to withdraws it!" And that's followed by a glare from her.

TUSHAR (smugly): "I'd prefer to take a *bike* instead with you holding me tight to prevent me from falling." as his friends applaud his response jocularly.

SUNNY: "But I do agree that love helps us tide over the greatest of pains in life" while the couples all coo together.

AVIS (mockingly): "But it also helps a bit if you look a bit more lovely!" as the men approve – cackling away.

AVISHKA: "Don't start that all over again, else you will have to spend more for keeping us that way!"

MANPRIT: "Seriously, you could really do with some of the treatment at home after undergoing a beautician course."

MAITRI: "Ok. But we don't really mind you guys going for it in order to put it in practice for us."

SANAA: "So that's settled then! We'll do the registration for you'll" and the ladies all cackle away.

MANPRIT (seriously): "We're NOT beauticians. We can do other treatments – though – like the *silent treatment* for which we've natural talent! But I do believe that it's only in adverse situations that pure love surfaces!" as the men now begin to laugh out aloud unabatedly.

TUSHAR (surprised): "You mean everyone else's love is impure?" while our friends are puzzled at his retort.

MANPRIT: "Well, it sure is diluted – what with all the materialistic presents. I think time and company is much more important than those intangibles!"

LYNDA: "I couldn't agree more! Maitri, you sure are a lucky woman" And suddenly she's embarrassed at all the attention coming her way.

SANAA: *"Kuch Seekho. Thoda romance seekho, Sunny* (Learn something. Learn some romance), Sunny!" and now it's Sunny's turn to feel awkward.

SUNNY: "Manprit sir, where can we 'find' and 'get' this pure love from?" while they all laugh out loudly.

MANPRIT (responding): "God has already given it to each and every one of us. You just need to be compassionate at all times, instead of being only passionate and that too very late" and our friends all burst out laughing at that amazing retort.

Despite what even the celebrated balladeer Bryan Adams had crooned – 'It's only love' – as a classic English duet song, there's a load more to life than just love.

One day, our friends found Harry discussing work travails privately with Tushar. They decided to get involved...

LYNDA (curiously): "C'mon Harry, out with it. What's ailing you?" while everyone was all ears.

HARRY (responding): "I'm really fed up with these incessant trainings in so many different programming languages" and all our friends smile away.

SUNNY: "Why so?"

HARRY: "It makes me feel like a blessed multi-lingual dictionary – like a Google or something!" And our friends laugh away.

MANPRIT: "So that's nice – isn't it?"

HARRY: "Really? And what do we do about that problem of getting confused in the syntax between multiple languages?"

TUSHAR: "True. Also, we tend to get mixed up with what we've learnt of an earlier programming language if we are deputed onto a project that doesn't require it."

LYNDA (advising): "How about practicing the earlier language occasionally to stay in touch?"

HARRY: "With our crazy schedules trying to keep exploring the newly learnt one, where would we have the time to keep up with the old ones?" And now everybody is in full support of his words.

SUNNY: "With the knowledge of so many languages, you could also become a 'Jack-of-all-trades' one day"

TUSHAR: "And become a master of none? No thank

you!"

HARRY: "How would you feel if you're made to re-marry once in every 6 months and also to support all the earlier wives?" And everyone was in splits at that repartee.

LYNDA (remarking): "I give up. I just can't seem to stop laughing at that analogy to be able to respond!" And our friends continue laughing away even more after that candid admission.

SUNNY (seriously): "Guys – I can understand that it's tough but it needs to be done. At the most, we can brush up faster with the unused when we need them rather than pick on them afresh" and now everyone finds that even more plausible.

TUSHAR (retorting): "I suppose you're referring to the ex–wives in question?" And everything else is drowned in the laughter that follows that remark.

11

TROUBLE IN PARADISE

Our friends relished the time to catch up with their families and other things during the slowdown. Gradually, things started to look up and they decided to catch up with each other again…

SUNNY (loudly): "Hey, things seem to be improving – miss weathercock – don't they?" as they all look towards Sanaa.

SANAA (smilingly): "I'm only a *fair weather* friend!" amidst roaring laugher.

MAITRI: "Good one, Sanaa" as they all agreed.

TUSHAR: "I think you need to get your eyes checked Sunny! She's not a weather cock, she's a hen."

SANAA: "I want no *cock* and *bull* stories here!"

AVIS (jutting in): "Guys-guys. Let's get the update first, shall we?"

AVISHKA: "Who's *Shalvi* here (shall we)?"

MAITRI: "Vishal's (we shall) sister!"

TUSHAR (trying to return to the topic): "Enough is enough! Let's get the facts right" and they all quieten down a bit.

HARRY (except him): "Of course. If enough isn't enough, then who else would be enough, *Eno?*" as some of our friends chuckle away – explaining it to the others.

HARSHITA: "Stop it right now, all of you! This is a serious matter" while by now everyone settles down to a more meaningful discussion at hand.

SANAA: "Well, the market definitely is getting better."

SUNNY (raising his glass): "Cheers to that!" as the others joined suit in raising a toast to a brighter future.

MANPRIT (relieved): "Feels so good to hear!" And everybody nods in appreciation.

AVIS (forewarning): "But we should still tread carefully for a while to set our houses in order" to the surprise of some of his friends.

MANPRIT: "Aye, Avis!"

TUSHAR: "Oh yeah! See how much I've pulled down due to reduced consumption!"

LYNDA: "Ya. I too have cut down –."

SUNNY (interrupting): "To size, you mean?" and they all

chuckle away while she frowns at him for that.

TUSHAR: "But you're already waif thin. Why in the world would you need to?"

LYNDA: "Would you believe there's something called 'leading by example', 'walk the talk'?"

TUSHAR (bowing down): *"Tussi great ho. Tumhare pair kahan hain* (You're great. Where are your legs)?" as our friends now burst out laughing at his approach.

LYNDA: *"Use charan kehte hain* (They are called feet)."

TUSHAR: *"Darshan honge tab to sparsh karenga na* (Only when we see them can we touch can them)."

LYNDA (uncomfortably): "Stop it, Tushar!" as their friends guffaw away.

TUSHAR (sarcastically): "Is that an (auto) rickshaw that I should stop it, one which you'd want to hail?"

LYNDA: "For your kind information, that's called to 'HAIL' a rickshaw. We only 'STOP' a vehicle when there's an emergency."

TUSHAR (saluting her): *"Hail* Hitler" as everyone including Lynda laugh out aloud.

And they disbanded for the night. Soon it was nearing the time for some other people to deliver the goods and they met up after a few months...

SANAA (enquiring): "Maitri, how are things

progressing?" as they all await her answer.

MAITRI (disclosing): "I have a few health issues but it's under control" and everybody is taken by surprise.

MANPRIT: "It's a real testing time!"

TUSHAR: "Spoken like a true *tester.*"

SUNNY: "How can you be so insensitive at such times, Tushar?"

HARSHITA (pacifying): "Don't worry, Maitri. You have all our wishes. Things will be just fine" as they all try to calm her.

MAITRI: "Thanks a lot, guys. It means a lot to me. Hey, how's yours shaping up, Harshita?"

HARSHITA: "So far so good. I throw up a lot and hence have a lot of moody blues…" the gals pity her situation.

SUNNY: "Tushar, now please don't ask her what she throws up!" as they laugh at Tushar.

TUSHAR: "Fine. I'll ask Harry, as he'll be the one doing the catching."

HARSHITA (shouting): "Just don't talk any shit, Tushar!"

TUSHAR: "Look who's talking. You're the one who has shit in your very name!"

HARSHITA: "Shut up, Tushar!"

TUSHAR: "Make that shit up! Now I know what you've been throwing up!" All our friends cackle out – as they try to visualize that.

HARSHITA (changing the topic): "Enough guys. And

what's your update, Avishka?" as their friends listen in.

AVISHKA (very curtly): "Nothing much" and everybody's surprised by that short answer.

SANAA (not accepting): "You mean you have NOTHING to report? How's that possible?" as they all shake their heads.

AVISHKA: "Guys, I don't want to talk about it" as her friends start getting worried.

HARSHITA (unable to see reason): "But why?" as they all await some answer.

AVISHKA: "Back off, NOW!" and her tone rattles our dear friends.

AVIS (restraining her): "Easy does it, Ave!" while they all look on puzzled.

SUNNY: "What happened here?"

AVIS: "She doesn't want to discuss it."

MANPRIT: "Is there a problem?"

AVIS (raising his voice over the murmur): "LEAVE it for now guys, please."

MAITRI: "We would really like to know, so that we can help out in some way."

AVIS (dejectedly): "It's already beyond that stage…" while that gets them all even more worried.

HARRY: "Now you're really scaring us!"

SUNNY: "C'mon guys. We're your friends. You can share whatever it is with us!"

AVIS (acceding to their attempts): "Are you sure you'll be able handle this?" And they all prepare themselves.

AVISHKA: "No Avis. Don't!" while Avis looks towards her as do all the others.

TUSHAR (reasoning): "Hey, don't hide it from us. We're only trying to help!" All of them try to persuade the couple to share the problem with them.

AVIS (regretting): "We just don't want to spoil your day!" And everybody assures him that it is more important to share it.

HARRY (forcibly): "What makes you think we'll let you take it all on your own. C'mon now – out with it!" as they all back him up.

MANPRIT: "Yes. We won't leave you alone until you part with your little secret!"

AVIS: "Well then – brace yourselves - Avishka's had a miscarriage" to the utter shock of everybody around.

AVISHKA (lowly): "This is probably the worst news I ever had. That's why I didn't want to share it and ruin your moods" and all the women rush to stop her from bursting into tears.

TUSHAR: "I agree this is a much crueler thing than the recession. But this too shall pass."

MAITRI (pointedly to her): "Oh you poor dear! Come here" while she hugs her tightly to comfort her after she tries unsuccessfully to put up a brave front and breaks down.

HARSHITA: "Things will be just fine. You'll get another chance!"

AVISHKA (strongly): "I don't think I can actually put myself through all that again!"

SANAA: "There's still a lot of time to go. As it is, you won't be up for it so soon."

MAITRI: "Yes. Just relax now and take it easy. Don't think of crossing the bridge till you reach it."

SUNNY (smilingly): "You can't *re-appear* this semester! You're late. Come back next year" as everyone smile at his attempt to lighten things up.

TUSHAR (continuing): "Prepare harder next year and you'll pass it with flying colors!" They all now began to see the funnier side to all the advice.

SANAA (chiding her): "You've *beaten* us to it though. We want a re-match!" Finally, she smiles as she realizes how hard they all have been trying to get her to come around.

AVISHKA: "I accept the challenge. You're on!"

TUSHAR: *"Aree...* (Oh) you people just don't know how to romance."

SANAA: "Looks who's talking. First hook up at least then start talking."

AVISHKA (snidely): *"Kunwara Baap* (A Bachelor Father)!" as they all laugh at that tag.

TUSHAR: "Exactly why I'm better, as I have to try *harder!*" and his friends are impressed by his confidence.

AVISHKA (taking him on): "Ok *guruji* (sir) – please give us poor souls one of your revered advices" while all our friends are excited at the prospect.

TUSHAR (issuing a sermon): "Sure – here you go…"

"Guys, please pay attention. I'll belt out a Hindi romantic song from the Bollywood movie *Kudrat*. Now you may have heard this before, but do watch out for the reaction."

LYNDA: "Good that you yourself gave us the warning so that we can brace ourselves," as her friends all laugh

TUSHAR: "You always under rate me, my dear. Let me prove you wrong…"

As he proceeds to sing:

"Tumhe hamse pyar itna (You love me so) –" while they were all listening in.

LYNDA (interrupting): "Stop. You got it all wrong!" and they all look in her direction, puzzled.

TUSHAR (replying): "Is it? Then show me the right way" as their friends await the correction.

LYNDA (demonstrating): "Ok. Here you go…"

As now she proceeds to sing:

"Hame tumse pyar kitna (I love you so)–" as her friends listen in attentively.

TUSHAR (interrupting): "Wow! I didn't know you too felt this way about me!" and now everybody burst out laughing.

LYNDA (sheepishly): "Oh shit!" while they all realize how he conned her into singing him a love song.

SANAA (applauding): "Congrats Tushar *guruji* (sir). You've made your point!" as all their friends are awestruck at the technique.

AVISHKA (teasing her): "Finally he's caught up with you, Lynda!" And they all cheer the couple.

TUSHAR (elatedly): "Please continue crooning, my dear!" while they all hoot at the couple.

LYNDA (embarrassed): "Not anymore. Please do the honors" as our friends laugh at her predicament.

TUSHAR (proudly): "Gladly. There's another more apt Hindi song now from the Bollywood movie *Kaamchor*. So here goes..."

He sings: "*Tum se badhkar duniya mein* (Better than you in the world),

Naa dekha koyi aur (haven't seen anyone else),

Jubaan par aaj dil ki baat aa gayi (Innermost feelings have come onto the tongue today)..." and they all clap along.

SUNNY (applauding): "*Nehle pe dehla* (One-upmanship)! Bravo" while they all cheer along.

MANPRIT (replying to Sunny): "You nailed it, buddy. But why not say tit for tat?" as they all laugh at his suggestion.

SUNNY (slyly): "The ladies will think we're getting physical!" And they suddenly get alerted to the possibility.

SANAA (angrily): "Whoa. The thought never occurred but now that you mention it, better watch out" while the ladies are all up in arms.

MANPRIT (bailing him out): "Let's use an eye for an eye instead. That's safer!" as the guys all laugh out and they pacify the ladies.

They wound up and left for their homes. Soon it was time for some more people to join this gang. However, they were too young to start working, so they made other people work around them. Our friends went to look up the new people at their current headquarters (the hospital where both the mothers were admitted).

TUSHAR (entering their room): "Many congratulations Maitri and Manprit on the newest addition to our group."

MANPRIT and MAITRI (smiling): "Thanks, Tushar."

SUNNY: "Congrats *yaaron* (friends). How are you coping, Maitri?"

MAITRI: "I'm doing ok."

SANAA: "Congrats M and M. That's great to hear."

MAITRI: "Thanks."

AVIS: "CONGRATS guys."

MANPRIT: "Thank you."

AVISHKA: "Congo. Now can we see the baby, please?

MAITRI (nodding her head): "Sure. It'll be back here shortly."

LYNDA (singing): "Congratulations and celebrations. (Now asking) So is it a he or a she?"

MANPRIT (smilingly): "Thanks. Why don't you guys take a count? Let's see who all are right" as they all absolutely gorge on the idea.

AVISHKA: "Why the suspense? And what if it's tied?"

AVIS: "As if it'll be both a guy and girl even if there's a tie."

AVISHKA: "Shut up, Avis."

MAITRI: "Quite possible even though you'll are most certainly very odd people" while they were confused whether to laugh at the last part of her remark or express surprise at her naivety.

AVISHKA: "By being possible, she means a tie – not both, as you so stupidly suggested, Avis. Now you see, you foolish fella, you were in – even thinking along those lines" and they all have a good laugh to a sheepish looking Avis.

MANPRIT (after counting the poll): "The majority of us say it's a boy."

AVIS: "Have you parents also taken part in the poll" as our friends all burst out laughing.

LYNDA: "So are we right or are we right?"

MAITRI (announcing the results): "It's a girl" to the delight of the winners.

AVIS (cynically): "So what are you trying to say? Do you mean that we're wrong?"

AVISHKA, SANAA and MAITRI (hissing): "Aavviiss" as he tries to hide behind a pillow.

SUNNY (curiously): "So what are you going to name her?" as everyone is eager to know the name of their newest member of the group.

MANPRIT (replying): "Haven't thought about that yet. Will decide later on" while Maitri mocks away at him even as the ladies start whispering a few names into her ears.

TUSHAR (sensing their uneasiness): "Great. You all relax. Meanwhile – guys – let's check on Harry and Harshita."

They all proceeded to meet Harshita and Harry…

TUSHAR (wishing): "Hearty congrats Harry and Harshita."

HARSHITA (pleased): "Thank you."

SANAA: "Congratulations Harshita and Harry."

HARRY: "Thanks."

SUNNY: "Congrats people. How are you Harshita?"

HARRY: "Thanks. Few problems but I guess things will be fine soon."

AVISHKA: "Firstly congrats. Now out with. Tell us what is troubling you?" as everybody listen in anxiously.

HARRY: "A couple of complications. But we're positive things will work out soon."

AVIS (relieved): "I'm glad. Hey congrats, dear friends. We'll be praying for you guys."

HARSHITA: "Hey thanks. That's so sweet of you, people."

SANAA: "Can we see the baby?" and our friends all line up.

HARRY: "It's under observation. It's a bit weak."

HARSHITA: "You will be able to hold it soon" while everybody is delighted to hear that.

LYNDA (excitedly): "Congrats. So, is it a boy or a girl?" as they all await the answer.

HARRY (smilingly): "Thank you. Why don't you'll take a guess while you're waiting to see it?" And their shoulders droop.

TUSHAR (dejectedly): "Not you too guys. Even the M-s kept us hanging awhile" as both the parents laugh at their friends' predicament even without *predicting*.

AVIS (sadly): "As it is, we won't be able to tell even when we hold it" as the parents see through his attempts to get it out from them and laugh at his effort.

SANAA: "Come on now – out with it. We can't bear the suspense any longer."

AVISHKA (overhearing the nurse): "Especially when we won't be able to see it today" as a hush of disappointment falls over the group.

HARRY (disclosing): "It's a baby boy" to widespread cheering in the group.

LYNDA: "Of course it's a baby. So what else can you call it – a *big* boy?" and her friends laugh out aloud.

AVIS: "So what's the name you guys have come up with?"

HARSHITA: "Well – it's too early for that. We will tell you'll once we have finalized" as they are surprised to discover that the parents have already shortlisted a few names without taking in their suggestions.

SUNNY (taking a cue to exit): "Take care. We'll try and catch the M's girl" while they all start making a move out.

HARRY (surprised): "Oh. You all still haven't seen her. Go on" as they all made their way out of their room.

They were finally able to see the little girl after the baby was fed when the nurse brought her to be with her mom for a few minutes. After meeting up with both their friend's families, they all went about their ways.

In a few days' time, both the mothers got discharged from the hospital and started resuming their routines handling the additional responsibility. Their friends dropped in after a couple of weeks at Harshita and Harry's home to check on how they were progressing...

HARRY (ushering them in): "Welcome guys."

HARSHITA (settling them in): "Yeah. Nice to see you'll."

LYNDA: "How are things, guys?"

HARSHITA: "Better."

AVIS: "That's good to hear. I see you'll have got adjusted to this stage."

HARRY: "Yeah. You tend to pick up the nuances gradually."

SUNNY: "Hey guys, where's li'l Harsha? (They had decided on the name of their little one)" They all looked around the place.

HARSHITA: "He's taking his nap and will be up soon" Everyone was delighted.

SANAA: "No wonder they look so adjusted – as they've got some time, now that he's sleeping."

HARRY: "Seriously. Precious little time before the little devil is up and active."

TUSHAR: "Looks like you're putting your paternity leave to pretty good use" and they all laugh away at that.

AVIS: "You still look as busy as you always have looked at work, except that this is a very different kind of work."

SUNNY (suggestively): "You can still work as hard as you ever have but with soft hands" while there were peals of laughter all round to that.

TUSHAR (chuckling): "Harry is now a househusband. Fits you, though" as his friends all laugh out loud at the insinuation.

SANAA (backing up Harry): "What's wrong with doing a few household errands?" and the women rally around him.

AVISHKA: "Good you're getting a lot of help, Harshita."

HARSHITA: "I just can't tell you how relieved I really am to have him around at this crucial time."

HARRY: "That's enough of that, Harshita. Harsha is 'our' baby."

SANAA: "So Harshita, does he clean up all the mess that Harsha creates?"

HARSHITA: "Not exactly. But he does help me out with some of the other household chores."

AVISHKA: "You should make him handle Harsha, so that he doesn't stick to you always" while the ladies agree on that one.

HARSHITA: "We've tried but he's frightened of his imposing dad."

SUNNY: "Must be because he always hurries things up and has the *harried* look."

LYNDA (shouting): "Hey – pipe down. See, we've woken up dear Harsha."

HARSHITA: "Not at all dear. He was due to wake up – in any case." They all make a dash for him, much to his shock – as the parents pacify him subsequently when he starts getting irritable and starts howling.

Initially – like all celebrities, Harsha got all the importance that he demanded, which he so rightfully deserved. He threw a lot of tantrums seeing so many people but gradually settled down. They all got so involved in playing with him that they didn't realize how late it had got, until he started puking out. That's when they saw Harry helping first hand – getting her the required things while Harshita proceeded to clean him up. The others too stepped in and assisted them to get things in order.

SUNNY (announcing): "Guys, I think it's time we made a move…" and they all started getting ready to head off.

AVIS: "Take care, guys. See you back at work soon."

TUSHAR (volunteering): "If you'll need any help, do let us know." The parents smiled in appreciation at the offer.

After exchanging pleasantries, they all left the new family to themselves and proceeded to their homes. Next week, they decided to check on Maitri and Manprit…

MANPRIT (welcoming them): "Hey guys, come on in."

MAITRI (pleased): "Wow. Good to see you'll."

SANAA: "How are you folks doing?"

MAITRI: "Fine."

SUNNY: "Wonderful."

TUSHAR: "Great. Where's our little … (recollecting) Maina (their child)?"

MANPRIT: "She's in her cradle inside, napping."

AVISHKA: "Nice to see you guys."

MAITRI: "Thanks. The feeling's mutual."

AVIS: "Yeah. We have been missing you guys, though."

MANPRIT: "We too."

SANAA (checking): "Maitri – have you been getting adequate assistance from Manprit?"

MAITRI (glowingly): "Oh yes. He takes a lot of care of Maina and frees me up for the other household duties" and the ladies are very impressed.

TUSHAR (confirming): "Oh – so does he cleans up all the mess, changes her clothes, etc.?" as they all eagerly await her response.

MAITRI: "Yes. He also takes care of her so that I get some time for us and also to myself."

SUNNY: "So a man has become a woman now!" while the entire guys laugh out loud but are forced to stop abruptly on seeing the scornful reactions on their respective partner's faces.

SANAA: "Nothing of the sort. In fact – if anything else – he's become a complete man" as all the women applaud.

SUNNY (smilingly): "You mean he wasn't one earlier?

Then how did he become a father?" and now all the men laugh more openly at that remark – not even bothering to look at their partners.

LYNDA: "What's wrong with doing the things that we do? If we wouldn't, you guys wouldn't have been able to even survive in this world, let alone arrive."

TUSHAR: "Manprit, it's a survival of the fittest – fear factor."

SANAA (: "He's doing a great job. Guys, learn something from him. Your time will also come."

MANPRIT (re-entering): "Here's Maina for you guys," and they all move their attention to their new little friend.

They all got busy trying to woo her, to win her attention and to win her over. Although Manprit went soft on her, she still played hard to get. Slowly, she chose whom to go to and everyone had a gala time playing with her. Only when she started behaving in a cranky manner did they realize that it had become rather late. They got to see Manprit in action as he tried to calm her down. Their friends tried their hands at trying to pacify her but couldn't succeed. Finally, Manprit stepped in and managed to put her to sleep...

AVIS (happily): "Guys, thanks for such a wonderful time. You must all be tired now." Both the parents smiled.

TUSHAR: "Yeah. I think it's high time for us to leave."

SUNNY (hugging): "Take care. Buzz us if you need anything," and the parents are happy with their visit and gesture.

After a few weeks, one of the new fathers began reporting for work…

TUSHAR (surprised): "Hey looks who's here – the hard working Harry" as they all look up from their desks to have a look at him.

SUNNY (welcoming): "Good to see you back, mate."

HARRY: "Glad to get back to work."

AVIS: "Didn't you have enough (work) at home that you wanted to do some here too?"

HARRY: "That work will also go on but we need to resume our routine work too at some point."

SANAA: "Are you fed up of *homework?*" as the ladies exchange smiling glances.

HARRY (vehemently): No. Not in the least bit!" But obviously, they refuse to buy that.

AVISHKA (suspiciously): "Did you have a fight with your better half?" as everyone awaits his response.

HARRY (replying): *"Nahi re baba* (Oh God, no)! I have exhausted all my 'p' leave and need to work in order to get paid" and now they understood the reason.

SUNNY: "Oh ho. No wonder you're looking exhausted."

LYNDA: "Why are you'll pestering him? He's trying his best to balance his personal and professional life."

AVISHKA: "When is Harshita reporting back?"

HARRY: "In a couple of months."

LYNDA: "Great. Wish her on our behalf."

AVIS (pointedly): "Hey, better keep a watch out. Your clothes are soiled with all the hard work that you've put in today" while Harry gets very conscious when all of them look towards his clothes in grave detail.

In the next few days, the 2nd new father also resumed work...

HARRY (announcing): "Guys – Manprit's back. Welcome bro" and all our friends were elated on seeing him.

AVIS (tugging his hand): "Hey, good to see you man."

MANPRIT: "Great to see you'll. How are you doing, Harry?"

HARRY: "Trying to cope."

SUNNY: "Welcome Manprit."

MANPRIT: "Nice to continue."

TUSHAR: "Hi bro."

MANPRIT: "God – I really missed you guys a lot
!"

SANAA (smugly): "Are you sure or you had too much of

baby time?" as the girls giggle away.

MANPRIT (emotionally): "I can never have enough of her, actually" and they all admire his approach.

AVISHKA (eagerly): "And what about Maitri?"

MANPRIT: "She'll join in 1.5 months" as our friends laugh at not only knowing that she'll be back soon but also on hearing that decimal answer.

LYNDA: "Will Maina be able to stay without you?"

MANPRIT: "I think Maitri will be able to hold fort till I return home."

SANAA: "Today must be tough on her, though."

MANPRIT: "I tried to help her by taking care of Maina till I started for here."

AVISHKA: "That's visible on your bag. It looks like the little one has initialed your stuff" while they all smile – seeing the food stains on his bag.

MANPRIT (brushing them off): "Oh. She was making a fuss when I was trying to leave – so had to feed her before leaving. Didn't realize I'd stained my bag. Thanks for bringing it to my notice!" They all laugh our aloud seeing his feeble attempts to wipe and even wash off the stains but to no avail.

Although the new dads had reported for work, the bigger reporting was at home to check on their beloveds throughout the day. They would both come in late or occasionally take a day off to help out. Work and even what they would wear and bring would suffer initially but they got the hang of it in a few weeks and would juggle both responsibilities. In about 2 months' time, the newbie moms started working and they were all back together. They had arranged for their parents and the crèche to take care of their children in their absence. After a couple of months, they had their routine business meet...

LYNDA (seriously): "We really need to complete the connections to those pipelines i.e. close those open deals..." while everyone listen on grimly.

SUNNY: "Yeah. They're so deep in the tunnel that we're *mining* them!" The others laugh a bit at his comment.

HARRY: "BTW – speaking of mines – that deal's mine!"

SUNNY: "Thank God we're no longer minors!"

LYNDA: "This is SERIOUS stuff – no laughing matter this!"

SUNNY (tongue-in-cheek): "All the deals are so slow-moving that all the effort behind pushing them through the tunnel is not visible!" Our friends cackle away at that.

LYNDA: "Signing up is the only and ultimate proof of securing a deal."

SUNNY: "With rationed budgets, it's difficult to get them to part with their money."

LYNDA: "They're in the rental era where they're merely

paying monthly. Just make them visualize how much they would have to pay up upfront as a one-time fee, if they were in the license period…" Everybody is suddenly thinking aloud.

HARRY (appreciating): "I like the idea. It's a very good cue!" And the friends are all impressed.

Soon it was time for them to wind off and head back to their respective places. Work went on as usual. Avishka and Avis slowly but surely had moved on to a new beginning as well.

Our friends were now troubled by some new winds of change that were sweeping through the industry and were gathering steam. It was the *storm* of automation that had taken them by storm…

TUSHAR (anxiously): "Man, this automated development is going to throw us out onto the streets!" Everyone eagerly listens in.

SUNNY (refuting): "These are early days. See how automated testing augmented the manual part and helped us to become more professional in our work." And our friends nod in approval.

HARRY (supporting Tushar): "We had developed automatic template generators for standardization purposes and Code generators will be able to create all the code completely by itself from the specs, even keeping them in sync at all times, which is tough for us

IT'S NOT ONLY LOVE...

to do."

LYNDA (adding to Sunny): "This myth isn't entirely true. It's like machines that produce goods replacing some workers. Still a few workers are required to check and sort the produce of the machines. Similarly, we will need developers to validate and finalize the output of such generators."

TUSHAR: "But still, it will drastically reduce if not completely eliminate the requirement of developers eventually."

SUNNY (countering): "See – as it is, supply of developers is vastly outstripping the demand for them, resulting in quite a few of them remaining unemployed. This is a step in the right direction to reduce the dependence on developers to create software so as to enable them to work on other aspects of software creation that can't be automated." Lynda gives him a look of approval.

LYNDA (summing up): "It enables the process of software creation to be sped up, as well as brings with it cent per cent accuracy" and now all our friends agree with her comments.

After a few months, Lynda set up a meeting with her friends, apparently to make an important announcement.

AVIS (egging him on): "Tushar – it could be the good news that you've been expecting" as they all truly believe that.

TUSHAR (excitedly): "Yeah man. I've been waiting for

her to come around for a long time. It's about time" and he waited with bated breath...

LYNDA (announcing): "Welcome ladies and gentlemen. Please settle down. Let's begin."

"As you'll are aware, business has slowed down a great deal. It has now started rapidly sliding downhill. We are moving towards the point of a standstill. Our present top line no longer permits us to continue with our existing scale of operations. We have to downsize right away to sustain our present bottom line. There are going to be widespread changes. At such times, some tough plans have been formulated – in the larger interest of ST – to stay afloat. This announcement should serve to prepare everyone for them and take suitable measures to deal with them. That is all I can communicate at this stage and will intimate those plans in the next couple of months."

"The announcement is over and done with and everybody can proceed."

Our bamboozled friends caught up in the canteen...

SUNNY (seriously): "With all the work drying up, this is bound to happen" and they began to realize the repercussions.

HARRY (dazed): "I never thought in my wildest dreams that it might be to discuss the turmoil" as they all agree.

MAITRI: "Let's brace ourselves!"

AVISHKA: "Looks like there'll be a breakaway."

MANPRIT (anxiously): "I'm really worried for our future," as everyone's busy contemplating about the situation.

TUSHAR: "I'm shell-shocked. It's has come down to the point of survival of the fittest"

AVIS (grimly)```: "Looks like a complete meltdown headed our way" as everybody is dead serious.

AVISHKA (resigned): "We'll have to start looking out" as our friends all nod in agreement.

After a few months, their worst fears started coming true as the situation worsened, and they met at the canteen...

SUNNY (taking a deep breath): "The future really looks very bleak now" and his friends all agree.

MANPRIT (raising his voice): "You're telling me? I've already put in my papers" to everyone's absolute surprise.

SUNNY (querying): "Why? Have you got something else lined up?" as his friends all await his response.

MANPRIT (defensively): "Maybe – in the near future"

and they're all confused.

SUNNY (asking): "Whoa. Is that a yes or a no?" as everybody await his reply.

MANPRIT: "Few things are being worked on. Nothing has been finalized just as yet."

SUNNY: "Well, at least you do have some options."

TUSHAR: "I've been asked to leave."

MANPRIT: "I suppose you have it covered."

TUSHAR: "Yes. I have some offers. Need to make up my mind."

MANPRIT: "Good *yaar* (dear friend)."

SUNNY (announcing): "I'm going, too!" This really shook them all up.

TUSHAR: "Now that's a shocker. Have you got something in hand?"

SUNNY: "*Na* (No). I'll take a little breather."

TUSHAR: "That's nice. Take some time off to rediscover your zeal."

SUNNY: "Ditto."

HARRY (concernedly): "What about you, gals?"

MAITRI: "I'm going too. I will fix myself something."

HARRY: "You sound as though you're going to make yourself a drink!" and our friends all burst out laughing.

SUNNY: "Good to have something to laugh about, after a while, at such serious times."

TUSHAR: "Harry – you seem safe."

HARRY: "Well – we're playing bombing the city and my turn will come too" while his friends all laugh away.

MANPRIT (dejectedly): "But it looks like the game is over. Our cities have already been bombed!" as they all shake their heads in pity.

TUSHAR (siding with him): "Yeah. We'll go out together." and they comfort each other in their hour of pain.

AVIS (joining in): "You bet man. Me and Avishka are also out" as they're pleased to know of their company and welcome the duo.

SUNNY: "No-no. The donkey always comes last."

AVIS: "She's already last" to peal of laughter all round.

AVISHKA: "Why, you creep!"

SUNNY (justifying): "The donkey means you – Avis. When we speak, we should always mention ourselves the last – just like when we count, we count ourselves the last" as they all chide over him.

AVISHKA: "Avi – first learn to speak, you gawar (illiterate)."

SUNNY (asking the A's): "Have you guys got something lined up?"

AVIS and AVISHKA (uttering alternately): "Neyn, Nie, Nedda, Nann" and our friends discover that they have nothing setup.

MANPRIT: "Oh shit. You better start looking out."

MAITRI (to Sanaa and Harshita): "Nice to hear that you gals are safe."

SANAA (analysing): "Good to see the A's, the H's and the M's are at least together. We will be separated – though but at least we have the H's right here beside us" while that makes their friends realize the line-up.

HARSHITA: "Why not go along with him, Sanaa?"

SANAA: "The money has to keep coming. Till he makes up his mind, I will hang around to support us."

TUSHAR (dejectedly): "This feels like just the classic Hollywood movie Titanic – a total disaster for most of us, except a few survivors – separated by that mountain of a woman" and they all see his analogy as well as the veiled shot at Lynda.

SUNNY (trying to lighten things up): "Harry – speaking of mountains – you'll have a hell of a mountain of work without all of us" while they all agree.

HARRY (pensively): "Yeah. Looks like I'll have my hands full with analysis, documentation, designing and testing too – to go with overseeing the development. But hard work never killed anyone..." as that makes everyone realize what it would be just like in a small company.

AVIS and MANPRIT: "Are you insured?"

HARRY: "Speaking of the trouble maker, where is she?" as they all start looking for her.

SUNNY: "She must've got held up somewhere on a call. She told me she's on the way."

LYNDA (joining them): "Somebody remembering me?

(Not getting any response but still continuing) Sorry guys I'm late. Nice to hear you'll are having fun in such adverse circumstances."

TUSHAR (bursting out): "Why did you have to do it? I'll always hate you for this!" as they all understood why he was so angry.

LYNDA: "Anybody else in my shoes would have to do the same dirty job."

TUSHAR: "But why did it have to be YOU?" and now his friends realize that he's heartbroken for what she had done.

LYNDA: "Don't look at it that way. It's the position – not the person."

TUSHAR (strongly): "You remind me of the tragic English song 'November Rain' from the amazing rock band Guns 'N' Roses, when things just all fall apart" while he surprises them all with his analogy.

LYNDA (defensively): "I'm helpless. What can I do? It's part of the job!" as Tushar shook his head vigorously.

MANPRIT (firmly): "From hired guns you've turned us into fired guns!" And some of them smile at the accidental humour.

SUNNY: "Like in that famous classic Hollywood movie 'The guns of Navarone." Only thing these guns are never on."

MANPRIT: "Now you'll get many tags like demolition

woman, one woman army and so on and so forth!"

SUNNY (attempting to pacify them): "Leave it. Let it go, guys" as they attempt to cool down their friends frayed tempers.

TUSHAR (cynically): "Why – I've even got something to give you for all you've done for us, Lynda" to everyone's surprise.

LYNDA (suspiciously): "And what's that?"

TUSHAR (handing her a packet): "It symbolizes what you should get – *ek anda (an egg)*, Lynda – on your bloody face!"

LYNDA (crying out aloud): "OMG!" and her friends are in a daze at that gift.

HARRY (supporting her): "Cool it – guys and take a moment to understand her plight, how difficult it is for her to see off her very friends" while a few of them mock him.

MANPRIT (aggressively): "Spoken like a true *chamcha* (loyalist)!" and they're all shocked at his retort.

SUNNY (stepping in): "Guys – let's not fight amongst ourselves" as he separates Harry and Manprit who nearly come to blows over their disagreement.

HARSHITA (supporting him): "Yeah. Let's part ways amicably – not like this" and they all make an attempt to keep cordial relations.

AVIS (joining in the melee): "Lynda – the liar, now on the prowl in her lair!" while some of them smile at the label as well as for the humor.

LYNDA: "Gosh – now WHEN did I ever lie?"

AVIS: "You never even told us you're gonna give us the sack!"

LYNDA: "Didn't I politely tell everybody to be prepared?"

TUSHAR (seething in rage): "Lynda – the *lynchpin* of the attack should be *lynched*" as their friends sense things are starting to get out of hand.

AVISHKA: "That's *enough*, guys! Please stop" and slowly they begin backing off.

MAITRI: "Let's swallow this like a bitter pill and move on" to which all the divided friends agreed.

SANAA (closing): "Yes guys. Let's not bring it to a point of no-return for this."

That said, done and dusted, for the first time, they hadn't parted ways happily – giving rise to two distinct camps! One-by-one they had to start leaving – their employments having being terminated. Tushar left in a huff followed by Maitri and Manprit in a matter of a few days. By the end of the week, it was Sunny's turn followed by that of Avis and Avishka in the next.

With the economy going into a downward spiral, none of them could take up any employment right away, even though some had options. While few of them focused on utilizing the time to do the things that they always wanted to but could never make time for, others frantically chased down all openings.

With a trimmed down company, Lynda had to shake up the hierarchy to fill up the voids created by the exits. Harry was elevated to the level of a Senior Manager. However, she was constrained to abolish the positions of Project Manager, Technical Architect and Solution Consultant besides the Graphic Designers, testing professionals and legal executives. As a result, more delivery accountability was passed on to her scle Manager and likewise more solution designing and development responsibilities to her Project and Team Leads. The requisite graphic designing, testing and legal roles were now fulfilled by outsourcing them.

The impact was demoralizing to the team where they began to visualize the yore years of working in smaller / startup organizations, coz the specialization was diminishing with reduction in the boundaries between multiple roles. She had quite a task on hand to prevent any possible exodus of her skeletal force but to her credit, she was not only able to keep them motivated but also performing. They took on the challenges and overcame them remarkably well.

———❦———

Summary

As they say – 'time & tide waits for no man'. This is life. We have a tendency to take things for granted, especially when they're going our way. Only when a fool & his gold are parted does a person realize what he's forgone. We should always keep things in perspective & see the bigger picture, rather than run after inconsequential stuff. Our voyage requires certain key things in good measure & we really need to ensure that we have enough of them to keep going. It needs to be given adequate time & space and those moments are to be cherished to help refresh the path. The only way that is possible is to keep creating memories – just like how Sunny had suggested in his early days, however big or small they may be, that will power us & will be treasured by us forever.

Now whats gonna happen to our dear friends, scattered away like never before? Is this the end of their journey together? Will they accept this reality – moving on – going about their lives or find some other method to it? Well, everything happens for a reason and their earlier experiences will certainly be put to use – when the time comes. For how long can they take it? Will they be able to go about the paces separated & leave all these developments behind them? Can they call a truce or quit? Can things really be sorted out?

Read on to determine and know more about their further lives in the upcoming sequel.

www.ingramcontent.com/pod-product-compliance
Lightning Source LLC
Chambersburg PA
CBHW021436020726
47499CB00006BA/2028